I0682291

IN YOUR BODY
IS THE
GARDEN OF FLOWERS

KINGSLEY L. DENNIS

Beautiful Traitor Books

Published by Beautiful Traitor Books –
http://www.beautifultraitorbooks.com/

ISBN-13: 978-1-9163268-8-0 (paperback)

Second edition: 2020
First published: 2013

Cover Concept: Kingsley L. Dennis & Ibolya Kapta

Cover Design & Book Formatting: Ibolya Kapta

FOREWORD TO THE NEW EDITION

This book first came into being around 2011-12. I do not have a clear memory of its precise inception date. It was first published in February 2013 – this I do know. The book was a kind of thought-experiment. It wasn't planned or scripted. I had no 'plan' for the book, or any idea of where it would take me. I took part in the book's creation as an equal participant. Both the stories in the book and myself travelled together, equally unknowing of the destination. Like I said, it was a joyful experiment and adventure.

The book was published quietly, with minimal formatting and little design. It was as if it ventured forth anonymously, with no announcement or recognition – a silent breeze through the garden. In hindsight, the book was not given its due.

Upon re-reading, I found the book to be a delight. I also feel it is more relevant now than upon its initial release. The main thread of the book talks about an 'Event' that took away so much from humanity – their memories, their joy and happiness, and the colours of the world. After the 'Event,' life is lived as if within a dehumanized dream. Yet around this narrative are woven a labyrinth of tales that all share their own colours and textures. In the original edition, I subtitled this book – 'A Tapestry of Tales.'

And within this tapestry, all the participants of these tales are trying to find their way home, in one way or another.

We are all seeking our way back home. These tales, as they weave in and out of one another, string together the beads of all our journeying and adventures. The one thing we should not forget is to keep a memory of the Way…

Kingsley L. Dennis

Casa Roja
Andalusia
May 2020

'A stolen kiss is not easily returned'

Saying

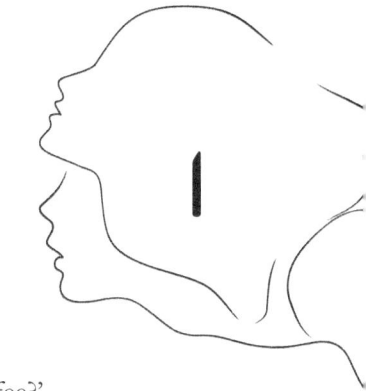

'What would you like?'

'Sorry?'

'What would you like - something to drink? Coffee?'

'I don't know. What would you suggest?'

'That depends on whether you are hungry or not. Are you hungry?'

'I don't know… am I?'

'How can I know - are you? Or are you thirsty?'

'I'm not sure what I feel.'

'Are you sure you feel alright?'

'This is really weird.'

'It sure is. Are you wasting my time?'

'Have we met before?'

'I don't think so.'

'Are you sure?'

'Pretty sure.'

'Would you know if we had?'

'I think I would. I recognise most of the faces around here, although there are less and less these days. Bad times you know. Well, I sure don't recognise yours.'

'Oh…that's strange.'

'Why is that?'

'I don't know how I know this, but…'

'Know what?'

'That I love you….'

2

It feels like there is no waking up. I pull the sheets away from me and I see a white canvas of light, as if another bed sheet had fallen over my eyes. I'm trying to find my way through to the next room, perhaps make a cup of coffee; to do something that will show me I am no longer asleep. But it's a sweet feeling, laying here amidst the soft warm waves of last night's sleep grooves. I feel the mattress is cradling me. Hard to move. Yet I must.

A soft haze hits me through the windows as I cross the floor. I move slowly…perhaps the body is inebriated with some dream filaments still clinging lazily to me like hungry creatures. Hazily I brew the coffee pot and sit down. Somehow, I know it's going to be a warm day. I stand up with the thought of pulling open the kitchen doors onto a bright outside. I do so, and a sudden smell of greenery and flowery stalks enters the nostrils. It's so great to be alive…or am I still dreaming?

'Excuse me?'
'Sorry?'
'I thought you said something?'
'No, I didn't.'

'Were you just dreaming then?'

'I'm not sure…maybe I was.'

'You need some more coffee?'

'Sure, fine.'

'Let me know if you want another refill.'

As the young waitress walks away from the counter, I notice a faint aroma of rose. Almost instinctively I feel that I should be here right now, as if being here counted for something. There's something in the rose that pulls my heart closer to the surface of my chest – just a fraction away from perforating the epidermal skin. Who is she? Words appear before my eyes in a deceptive vision – *'All things shall come to you who are awake – so awaken…'*

There is movement around the café; ghostly figures of varied hues…I see the colours glide past in streaks like a tapestry being woven around me. A tapestry of scenes and histories all occurring simultaneously; in each instant a thousand melodramas. Not in time but in essence. I cannot yet see clearly. Too many blurred outlines. I look into my coffee cup at the dark liquid as I feel bitter fibres in my throat. I long for something that calls to me in that waitress. It's maddening. It's illusive. There is a longing mixed with the taste of some unknown fear.

I look over at the counter. She is not there. I get up slowly and move towards the door that leads into the back kitchen. Just as my hand reaches out for the door, I hear her voice. I turn slowly to see her standing a few feet from me. I could not hear what it was she said.

I pass through the door with an odd feeling. I am trying to remember her words. What does she reveal to me? I turn slightly, yet she does not follow. She stays as if on a threshold just beyond…and I have passed through.

The door swings closed behind me to reveal a brightly lit kitchen. There is no-one here, and the light is too bright for me. I feel disorientated and senseless. I force a gaze around and see the outline of a door at the far end of the room. I move towards it feeling a need to reach it either before something obstructs me, or I forget myself and become lost. I reach it and open the door. Outside a garden stretches away. Before me, a soft glow sprinkled between the steadfast trees. I enter and make my way down a path towards a central clearing where a stone fountain gushes water. But I'm not thirsty and can still taste the coffee in my mouth. I sit upon the low stone wall of the fountain and listen to the water splashing.

3

Sprinkles of wet spray touch my skin and rest gently upon my arm. Each touch dissolving between the hairs that dampen slightly. With each gentle spray upon the skin it feels as if the body is gradually disintegrating into light. From the interior of my form, where blood and desires mix like flittering fishes, a flame of scarlet rises up like fiery water. I am an ocean where all yet none swim. I am a gestation pool of unformed yet eternal thoughts. There is a moment within endless moments where waking life seems but a blur of imaginal pictures that become everyone's dreams. And as suddenly as this fleetingness began, so it does dissipate into rapid air. None of this is real, and yet nothing feels untrue. There never was a love; and yet there never was a time where love did not exist. There never was a light that lingered, fermenting my longing. Or there never was a place where light could not go.

Yet I am missing something. It is so obvious and yet there is no trace around me. No tatters of some wedding gown, passion ripped.

I stand up and will my body to move away from the fountain. I walk around its low perimeter wall, knowing that it does not allow me entry. I circumnavigate like a haunted sailor. After a three-quarters circling of the fountain I see a door set in the wall that encloses the clearing. Without forming a thought, I move towards the door and reach for the old iron handle that soundlessly turns in my hand. The door springs open towards me without friction. I peer inside and wait as my eyes accustom to the unexpected darkness.

I am in a small room. Across from me in the corner is a desk. The desk looks cluttered; many dishevelled papers and books piled high. The scene clears, like the beginning of some play, and a figure walks into view. It is an old man who shuffles over to the desk and sits down, then ruffles through some papers like a tree-top breeze. There is near complete silence except for the sound of rustling paper-leaves that begin to entrance me.

'You came so you should stay. That is the way,' said a voice from behind the papers. I look up into the old man's face for the first time. It is aged and grey, with a small goatee beard, yet vibrant like a shiny new toy.

'We are here because there is work to do – both work within you and work within me. Because of this we have such a thing as love. Without love there can be no real desire for the movement towards the beginning,' the old man continued.

'Beginning?' I ask, with a hushed voice.

'You look and sound as if you are lost somewhere, rambling through your dreams. Remnants of some love, perhaps?'

'Are your words easy?' I found myself asking.

'As easy as your emotions,' replied the old man.

'My emotions tell me I need to be here,' I said.

'Your emotions tell you nothing of the sort; this is your big, fat ego speaking. Your emotions are wrapped up in balls of saccharine. You are a walking shell of incomplete unknowns.' The old man raised an eyebrow and half-smiled. I walk towards him and feel compelled to kneel at his feet.

'If this is so, then where is the true beginning?'

'If you knew,' began the old man, 'you would not be here. It all begins in the asking; the capacity to ask. There can be no movement without intention. You are in my land now, and here laws operate differently. Remember that everything is different out here. It all works differently once you pass the threshold. Never forget that what keeps you here will not keep you there. Remember this…'

And this is where it began. Yet I never forgot how the coffee tasted in my mouth for there still reverberated within a scent of some love.

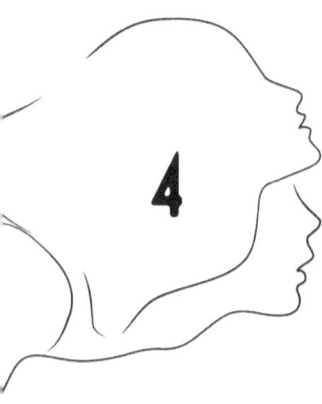

4

The morning light shone through the windows as does a hand that shakes a sleepy body. Daylight entered like an honoured guest and rested gently upon the room. I awakened refreshed yet strangely absent to myself, as if I had left so much behind. Now all I carried was my skin, hanging softly in folds like thin curtains. Somewhat relieved that whatever had been so real to me was now leaving me alone, I felt free of debt.

I left my small room with vestiges of some memory of the old man with the face of the moon. I entered what I thought to be the room of the previous evening only to find myself in the front room of a small cottage. It seemed to be the largest room and contained a rectangular wooden table in the middle. At the end of the room was an open fire, with what looked to be pots and pans for cooking. And there along one wall was an area for food preparation, and a sink. Suddenly the main door opened a young girl walked in carrying a pot.

'Father, you are awake. Is it not late for you?' said the young girl casually as she passed me. She must have been no more than eight or nine years of age, with dark hair tied into a pigtail; a kind yet intense young face. She was a pretty girl with an aura of movement, of action.

'I was tired,' I said absently.

'You can still chop some wood before the food is ready,' she answered.

'And you will cook?' I asked.

'Yes father,' she replied, and started to pour the pot of water into a bowl near the fire, not turning to look.

Instinctively, I walked towards the door and stepped into the outside world; a forest of morning sounds and unusual smells.

Picking up the bag of tools laying at the entrance I began to walk down a path that led into the forest. I was a woodcutter. The sense of remembrance was strong in me. Instinctively, I knew the role allotted and what to do. I felt an attraction to this work and hurried my steps expectantly. And now it was not just for myself – I had a beautiful daughter to look after.

I worked hard all day to chop wood; to cut it into firewood and tie it into bundles. I laid the bundles of wood beside me on the forest floor. I longed for fresh pools of water…pools for looking and for laughing into. I wanted to look into these watery mirrors and to find the answers to questions long hidden in the unreaches of my collective memory. I was now a man of action – a woodcutter – yet still missing knowledge. I felt within me traces of the love a father often wishes for. In my daughter I had an unspoken connection; yet there were spaces of unfulfilled longing, where thirsty dreamers come to quench their dry throats. My throat was so dry I could have drunk a mountain of dove tears.

The forest around me was beautiful, like unspoilt imagination, and was soothing in its peace. Into this I was surely the intruder. I was no longer the navigator, the voice, the captain - and certainly not the commander. If anything, I was the lost wayfarer, walking the threads of a long absent Ariadne.

I returned to the cottage with a bundle of firewood as the sun was setting, with a light wind rising behind me like an ancestral voice. My daughter welcomed me with expedient grace and warm food as promised. It was a cosy relationship, a dance of human bonding, blood, and necessity. I ate heartily.

'Father?' said my daughter as we had finished eating. I looked up into her eyes with a silent face. I was still thinking, repeating to myself that I was a woodcutter, and believing in the entanglement of words. Suddenly, the reverie was broken, followed by a humming pause.

'I wish that we could have different food,' she said after the short lull. I looked at her expectantly. 'We eat the same food day after day; is it not time we had other types of food to eat? I'm bored of the same old food. Father?'
'Yes, you are right' I murmured instinctively. 'We should be having different kinds of food by now. Tomorrow, I will get up early and go deeper into the forest to cut a second large bundle of wood, which I shall cut and shape into firewood and I will take both bundles of wood into town after breakfast. I will sell this firewood for good money and bring us back both different kinds of food to eat.' I spoke in a decisive tone.

The next morning, I awoke before dawn. That night I had slept well and deep, with no unearthly adventures. This was unusual, for my nights were often filled with the vicissitudes of dream fragments; such flickering, fleeting encounters that one could hang on a wall of pictures upon awakening.

Alone, I drank coffee whilst my daughter slept, coddled and cradled by her own desires and dreams. The coffee tasted deep, bitter, and strong. Its aftertaste reminded me of some longing I could not recall. Some place I had perhaps once passed through amid some history that was not mine, and yet was.

5

I raised my head up from the counter and refocused onto the scene before me.

'Did you sleep?' asked the waitress

'No. Why – do you think that I did?' I answered blankly.

'You looked as though you did. Were you tired?' she asked.

'Yes. I'm tired. I feel tired all the days now. I don't know why,' I said as I drank from my coffee cup. The waitress smiled and turned away. I did not want her to leave. She was a thread to some place, feeling, longing I could not trace. She was an ancient myth, a thread that I somehow had lost and must regain.

'I don't know how but I know I love you,' I whisper under my breath.

The waitress turned into the kitchen and was gone. I stumble out of my chair and walk towards the door she exited. I'm moving slow despite the sensation that all time and motion around me was accelerating. It is as if I am losing time. I reach for the door that leads into the back kitchen. I pass through it and emerge into a brightly lit kitchen. There is no-one here. I gaze around and see a door at the far end that is slightly ajar. I walk towards it with my heart beating rapidly in my chest. I am hoping I will not awake before reaching the other side of the door. I lunge and I am through the door. I am standing in the middle of a forest. My love is gone, and I am left beguiled.

6

I worked hard to cut a large bundle of wood which I trimmed into firewood. Returning to the cottage, it was still very early. The sun had barely had time to rise over the roof of trees, bathing lightly the covering of leaves, the caress of veins through Nature's canopy. In a walk that was slow, timed to a pace outside of normal acceleration, I brought the bundle of wood back to the cottage and, finding the front door locked, I sat down next to the wood. Perhaps my daughter had gone out for a walk, locking the door behind her in her forgetfulness? Despite these mental roamings, I soon fell asleep.

Waking up to a sun that was already high, I knew it would be too late to go into town to sell the wood at market. Such rituals of buying and selling had been instilled into the social mores and practices of local habit much like wood has its line of grain. Following the line of the sun I retreated back into the canopy-shade of the forest, wandering deep into the hills to find better firewood. So too had the ritual of collecting firewood become an essential act of human survival - bringing warmth into the shelter and habitus of the human. Through the control of fire humankind had kindled their way into partial, uncertain futures. With ever-greater uncertainty I moved forward through the throng of forest, with its native wildlife and living form. More work to accomplish before my day was done.

I worked hard all day without any food until I became cold and hungry. I was being driven by some desire, or need, to fulfil, to provide, and to accomplish. I was hungry for some kind of recognition I had been denied or felt I had been denied. Love, in some form or other, was scattered about me in all the obstacles, objects, and events that crowded into this thing called my life. And in the distraction of some love my daughter had been conceived and born into this world. Yet, for the origin of that love, I was now blurred and forgetful. Somehow, I must have gone astray, like some lost animal after the rains; a scent, a trail, washed away by a watery hand that sweeps the path to one's own past. Some taste remained, however, and it mingled softly, and subtly, with the buds at the back of my throat. I moved on, the bundle of wood on my back, hungry now for different foods.

Arriving back at the cottage the day had fallen into darkness and stars were now sprinkled above as distant isotopes upon an unknown blackness. Finding the door locked I knocked, and knocked again loudly, with no answer being returned to me. The cottage was a closed shell, with its life beyond the few inches of threshold barred to entrance. It felt to me as if I had been suddenly excluded and thrown out of my own life's role like an actor is fired from the stage. In the midst of a dark and cold night I stretched my head back, raised my arms wide, and breathed in heavily and deep, drinking the raspy crispness of the air and sinking into a heart-weary reverie. I began to float.

I floated through the sea of stars like some ancient mariner, or like an unfinished craft of the gods. Weaving a path through the firmament I sensed the energies of the stellar beings around me, a trespasser in the garden of nakedness and light. Here no beginning was conceived, and no end was in thought. Time was not present and neither did it critique. Linearity of thought and action was alien in this place that I drifted through. I felt that I was a fractal in the infinitesimal, outside of birth and death.

Then a seed of thought hit me from an unknown depth. I was a receiver, scrambling madly for signals, for clues to arrive. On cue the programming reached me and jolted my presence into a sudden awareness that lasted no measure of calculable time. Another moment was awaiting.

Love, were you awaiting or releasing me?

7

The market bustled and jostled with the smells and sounds of careless interaction. People mixed like gaseous atoms in some osmotic mist. There was a myriad of destinations yet only a handful of intentions. The humming of human buzz hung over the market like fine rain, touching the cheeks of everyone who milled and hovered. I felt a stranger and yet no-one paid me any attention as if my presence were of no care. Beside me my bundle of firewood lay upon the ground as I stood rooted to the spot. Lamp-like I remained a sorry beacon in a world where no light was requested or called-forth. Forlorn and unsure I picked up my bundle and wandered around the market in a daze. Occasionally, the smells would seep into my nose and invade my harassed senses. Like a sanctuary for intruders, I was being assailed in both my outer and inner worlds.

I made my way through the throng of barging bodies. This was pure mediaeval. This was some history that was not yet completed. As if living in another timeline where I was still yet seeking for some love incomplete. Was this my way of cleansing some past that was stuck, lodged somewhere within the multiplicity of my souls?

I sold the wood for a good price to an old man with a kind face.

'Have you heard of the Master Storyteller?' asked the old man.

'No', I said, 'who is he?'

'He is the remover of all difficulties, and his tales exist in all times and in all places - as long as there are people in this world to hear them!' said the old man, his eyes glinting like gems.

'Will his tales remove my difficulty?' I asked.

'Maybe they can,' replied the old man.

'And how do I find this Master Storyteller?' I asked with a longing in my voice.

'If you need enough, and yet want little enough, you shall find the food of your soul,' the old man said as he walked away with an enigmatic smile. The smile faded into the distance long after the man had gone. Now the old man had become a part of the buildings and stonework as if he had only been a manifestation of my imagination. An image that lingered too long in doorways where my own look should not reach. Where should I find this man, this Master Storyteller?

Do not let me linger too long within the realm of the invisible where the heart lies fleeting!

With the money from the wood I booked my own bed for the night in some caravanserai; a house for traders who live for the barter of the road. I was sleeping amongst the finest storytellers who travel from place to place with a story to tell, a tale to sell, and the fantastical to beguile you with. I was like a leper in their company, maimed by the onslaught of the enchanted. At night, when voices became as murmurs upon the breeze, this fine company of charlatans and mystics would bend their bodies around the caravanserai fire to release their tales. They spoke of djinns, demons, fairies, fire-sprites, and treasure. With tongues laced with liquid gold they became the alchemical brothers of myth. Like true troubadours they became the heralds of deeds long done and hearts long pierced by the fiery lance. Their words acted upon my own leaden heart, slowly kneading it as if it were like quicksilver and their stories the heated crucible.

I could not resist returning to this den of mystique. Night after night I would return to hear these tales after a long day venturing far into forests to find my firewood. I sold my trade to heat others' homes whilst my own hearth lay cold. If it were not for these nightly tales, I believe my inner flame would have perished and my heart fractured into embers. The storytellers changed as the caravans moved on, yet the tales continued to arrive like living substance. As a trader one night remarked under the dying flame of the fire – 'my friends, the dog may bark but the caravan moves on.' Indeed! We ragamuffin company all nodded our heads, as if we were all bound by some unspoken conspiracy.

The days passed with onerous work. Early mornings in the forests cutting wood and shaping the pieces into bundles of firewood. The trees bent heavy and brooded over me as I felled their kin to comfort mine. To reciprocate I would often repeat the tales from the night before to my wooden audience. Then a long afternoon spent trudging the bundles of wood back to the marketplace to participate in the throng of trade. It earned me little, yet it earned me enough. My physical body grew under the strain until my sinews were taut and healthy. Many women eyed my physical shell as it pressed against the frail fabric of my outer garments. Yet they knew not that I was but a pauper inside this shell. I felt like my pearl had been stolen by some sea-urchin long ago. I ate enough to keep my limbs strong, and fed my mind with the caravanserai tales. My heart starved and grew thin.

On the eve of the summer equinox a crowd had gathered in the caravanserai to hear a renowned man speak. His name, I learnt, was Babu. From afar he had travelled and yet no-one knew from where. He appeared after his renown had reached the town. He was, it was told, an itinerant mystic who walked between both worlds. Was he to be the Master Storyteller? Interest in his arrival was rife and men brought their male children to sit at the feet of this sage. A larger than normal fire was made and later that evening as the sun had slid beneath the horizon on its dawnward journey, we sat amidst the flames. I crouched in anticipation, eager for my difficulties to be removed by tales.

The man known as Babu was darkened of skin and ruddy in looks. A face that had faced many a night under open stars. From under dark eyebrows he pierced his gaze through the crowd like a lighthouse scans the seas. When he came to my eyes, he hesitated a deliberate moment and sank some hand into my soul. I felt as if fingers were scraping around for something that wasn't there. I felt guilty and looked away, and scraped the dust before me with the same tawny fingers. Then a voice strong and deep began to tell a tale.

"There was once a King named Ahmed Bakht who was a most generous ruler. Under his generous rule the kingdom far and wide prospered, and the King's empire flourished and grew happy. Yet the King himself was not happy, for he had borne no son and thus no male heir to his throne. One morning whilst gazing into the splendour of his golden mirror his eyes rested upon a single grey hair in his beard. 'Oh Lord, it has come to this,' wailed the King in his grief. 'I have everything and yet I have nothing for there is no-one to succeed me and retain my legacy. Like this grey hair I too grow old and grey. Has my life achieved nothing?!'

In great distress the King threw off his robes and entered his private prayer chamber. He gave orders to his ministers and servants that he was not to be disturbed. He was, he said, renouncing the world and retiring into contemplation.

Wearing a cloth of simple cotton, the King withdrew from the world of empires and armies. He renounced all his powers and gave rulership to his loyal Vizier who had served him faithfully all his years. Consuming only water, bread, and dates, the King sank into his heavy heart. He passed his days as a drowned King; his kingdom a water-world to him. Yet when the rest of the empire heard word of the King's strange state, rivalries between local rulers broke out. Skirmishes and scuffles turned usurpers into violent local rulers. The kingdom was beginning to splinter from the inside out. Once promised loyalties faded into worded remnants. The sacred became tarnished with the profane as there was no King at the head of the table.

One day the King's Vizier – a wise and trusted servant – entered the King's private chamber without invitation. With supplication he approached the ragged and bedraggled King. The Vizier was surprised to see the taut face of the once glorious King. His eyes sunken into his head like a pair of scared creatures.

'Oh, my dear and respected King,' began the Vizier, 'it is also because I have been your loyal and devout servant for so long that I do ask your forgiveness for this intrusion. It is because of my respect for you, and our lasting friendship, that I do now speak these words to you. Your kingdom is falling apart; your provinces vie for power; and war begins in earnest over your lands. Your beloved empire is without a head, and so now flails and writhes in headless confusion. Is this God's will? Did God place you in this sacred position for you to abandon it and to fail his people? Are you ruler over people and lands so that you can abdicate your responsibility? Whatever your personal grief, this is nothing when compared to the grief of God over your desertion. Your presence is desperately needed; this is your responsibility and for you alone to carry. Please, I beseech you, do not turn your back upon your own Path because of one grey hair.'

With these words the body of King Ahmed Bakht trembled. 'My dear old friend, I cannot thank you enough for these words! You were right to admonish the foolish old man that I am. I have a kingdom to rule - how neglectful I have been!'

King Ahmed Bakht returned immediately to his throne and summoned his ministers, courtiers, and guards to his council. New decrees were sent throughout the land and upon the acknowledged return of the King order was once again established within the kingdom. Yet the King was not the same man he once was. Although still generous and benevolent, he now showed more humility. Ahmed Bakht had realised that there was still so much he did not know, and that he was so far away from having even a cupful of wisdom. So, one day the King decided to make a secret trip in the dead of night to the shrine of a local sage. Yet after thinking that it would be unwise to arrive in full fanfare with an entourage of servants and guards, he resolved to go in disguise.

One night soon after, when the moon was at her lowest ebb, the King dressed in rags and carried a lantern through the streets. He walked past the town walls and into the realms of Nature where an eerie wind blew through trees and grass. Yet on the way to the shrine a gust of wind blew up and extinguished the flame of his lantern. A little scared, the King groped in the dark for a way. Seeing a glow in the near distance, and thinking it be a lantern hanging over the sage's shrine, he crept forward. As the King approached the light, he saw four robed figures seated around a fire. The four figures were dressed in the patched robes common to dervishes. Yet the King, in his caution, could not be sure if these were indeed dervishes of the road, or robbers concealed as such. He crept forward in stealth and hid himself behind some near bushes, in the hope to catch their conversation. A voice rose like smoke from the fire as one of the dervish figures spoke:

'Oh, brothers of freedom, brothers of the open road, have we not assembled here tonight to share our company? Who knows what tomorrow will bring, whether we continue together or part forever never to reunite? Our destiny is as yet still unknown. Let us pass our time tonight in some delight – let us each tell our story for others to remember?'

King Ahmed Bakht leaned forward to hear the first dervish as he cleared his throat to speak.

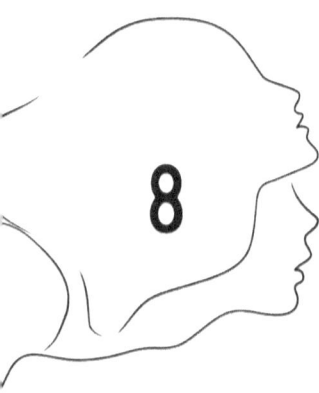

8

I am awake and lying in my sister's bed. Her soft silk sheets wrapped around me like a coating of betrayal. The room is lavish and scented with jasmine. I am so ashamed. I have nothing now except my regrets; they hang like frozen tears from my cheeks. I have been ravished and robbed of all my wealth and esteem through my own acts of wanton foolishness. I lie like a thing broken, a life unspoken.

The tragedy of our parents' untimely death left me with a wealth that was unexpected. With my sister married and living away I became heir to a business fortune. How this unfortunate turn of events did bring with it its own share of misfortune. Sorely I was tested - and found wanting. Lavish parties were thrown in honour of friends who had pledged their brother-blood for me, and advisors crammed by inexperienced ears with selfish plots and betrayals. The business I had inherited became neglected and mistreated. In short, I was robbed by those closest to me whilst I lay lured like a pussycat into a thieves' den. Hedonism beguiled me with pleasure and distraction, and I courted the realm of my higher class. I should have known how out of place I was, and yet I must have been easy prey. For when the business lay ruined and my money spent, those brothers who once pledged their blood for me avoided me like the Black

Death. What a fool!

Only the kindness of my sister saved me: true blood. I came like a beggar. I who had ignored her calls and letters when I was in pleasure; now in destitution when I called, she embraced me warmly. And here I now lie, cleaned and well-nourished in her own dwelling.

'Brother, I trust you have regained your strength and are feeling well?' asked my sister as she entered the room. She laid before me a tray of finest fruit.

'Yes, thank you dear sister. Your kindness has touched me. I feel ashamed for what I have done. So much squandered in so little time.'

'These are the ways of the world for which you are not well-suited to,' replied my sister with a kind smile.

'But what must I do? I cannot lie here forever!' I exclaimed.

'True. People will speak badly of you, saying you now squirm off the earnings of your brother-in-law. You need to raise yourself again.'

'Yes, I know. How should I do this?'

'I will provide you with some money to buy some quality merchandise here. I know someone who often transports cargo from city to city. Go on ahead to the great citadel over the sands and re-make your fortune.'

'Sweet sister! How can I repay you?' I cried with joy in my frail voice.

Strange how times can move like little sea creatures. Fluid moments connected like seahorses pushed by the ebb; their colours flashing by.

It was dark when I arrived at the gate of the citadel. Knocking, the gatekeeper opened the barred window and asked curtly of my need.

'I am here as a merchant. My goods will soon follow. I am to establish my trade here,' I replied.

'No entry after dark. You must wait it out until morning.'

'What? But I have nowhere to stay – it is just desert and sands here. There are thieves and brigands!' I replied nervously.

'That is as it is. And those are the rules. You can come in at first light.' The little window hatch closed as if it were my last portcullis of hope.

The night wind chill coated me as a second skin. I sat forlorn with my head between my knees. I wondered whether fate had some intention for me – was I being pushed around some ethereal checkerboard? I had moments to spar with my past deeds, my back against the citadel wall. Until now my youthful head had ruled all my actions. I had rationalised everything to justify my desires and greed. Materiality had become its own quagmire to me. I now wished for change. I longed for a change of mind. Indeed, to push my thinking downwards from the skull to my fleshy heart.

No sooner had this thought become grounded in me that I noticed not far from where I sat a chest being lowered over the citadel wall. Was this some food and clothing from the god of travellers? I cautiously approached the chest. It rested silently upon the sands, wooden and yet like stone. Opening the lid, I saw the blooded beaten body of a young lady, slumped in redness and deathly. Her eyes could barely open, and yet in their sorrowful state was sensed the spark of beauty. Bewitched I leant forward to hear a whisper upon her lips.

'Bury me beneath the sands so none shall know of me. I judge not my killer.'

Astounded at such gentleness in death, I cowered over the broken body and did my best to comfort her. Until morning broke did I guard this chest, then ran crazed to the door to ask for permission once more. I hurried inside the citadel and hired men to help me carry this wooden casket to newly acquired rooms. Immediately, I enquired after the most proficient doctor of the town to come and tend to this lady.

The story I gave was that my wife and I were attacked by brigands outside the citadel, and my wife beaten near to death. And for a month this situation remained. The good doctor attended to this lady daily as she lay incapacitated in bed. And daily I was witness to her beauty returning. Like an orchid blossoming this young lady came back into the sun. Soon my own goods arrived at the town and I was once again able to trade and to repay all debts. In these endeavours I made good fortune and thus was able to give my new lady friend the finest treatment available. I withheld no money in her treatment. For truth be told, I was now in deep love with this mysterious lady.

'I ask of you nothing,' she would often remark. Frequently followed with 'do not look at me; neither of us is worthy.' What is to be worthy? Where is it written that beauty is not to be gazed upon?

Both my waning hours and my money I did spend on her presence. Smitten like a love-dog I wagged after just a look from her. Though she did not engage me in friendship or conversation I gloried just knowing this lady dwelt in my house. I lost interest in my trade and failed to find new stocks and to replenish. Once my old stock was sold, I began to drift, not knowing what shore I was heading towards. Thus goes the fate of dreamers!

Noticing the predicament of my affairs one day the young lady gave me a letter and told me to deliver it to a nearby address. Opposite the citadel palace I found this small holding and delivered the unopened letter to the servant. Upon a short wait the same servant returned with several bags of gold and bade me leave with these. Again astounded, I returned to my lady with this new fortune. What game was being played out upon the chessboard of our lives?

At the lady's request to bedeck her in fine jewellery I sought out the finest jeweller of the town. It was a handsome shop indeed. Filled with the finest jewels and sparkling gems I procured the best to return with. The young man of the shop was most pleased with my purchases.

'I can see you are a man of distinction and taste. And of tales too no doubt! Stay here and share food and drink with me, I insist!' It would have been rude to dismiss such hospitality, as it sustains many a transaction in these times. We moved on through to a palatial garden, a cornucopia of plants and fauna courted by soothing fountains and bird songs. It was certainly a walled garden of delight, shaded from the midday sun. And in these splendid surroundings did we eat and drink. Yet all the time I remained careful not to divulge too much of my own personal circumstances. I felt I was harbouring my own cautious mystery.

Soon a spell of sadness befell the face of my new young friend. He appeared to become agitated and restless.

'What ails you friend?' I asked in genuine concern.

'I find it difficult to gain pleasure without the presence of my beloved. I need her to sit at my side,' said the young jeweller in obvious distress.

'Then call her here to join us. I do not mind if our intimate circle is expanded,' I said. For sure, to me it was no issue to have a woman join our midst. This immediately seemed to brighten up the young man.

'I shall call her at once; thank you friend for your understanding!' And a servant was dispatched to bring the young jeweller's beloved to him.

As the young man's beloved entered the garden I was shocked by her hideousness. What a hag! Her old wizened face was festooned with pock marks and blotches and her straggly hair hung greasy and grey. Could this creature really be the beloved of my youthful companion? And yet it was so! On meeting this pair embraced and kissed like fondest lovers. The sight was distracting and distasteful to me, yet I could not part. I remained in their company until polite hospitality ran its course.

On returning to my own beloved I begged her forgiveness for being away so long.

'I do not require your constant company,' she said in a voice that neither encouraged nor deterred me.

'True. And yet I feel I fail if I am not here to protect you constantly,' I protested.

'Protect me from what?'

'From that which wishes to harm you,' I said.

'And which is that? If I am a victim of life or love, then it is my own undoing,' she added before turning away.

Oh, my beloved, do not turn away. Do not cast your face in shadow; I long to be burned by your look.

The next day, at my lady's insistence, I returned to my young jeweller friend to return the hospitality and invite him to our residence. I was surprised to the extent that my beloved became animated by the new activities. She busied herself like at no time before to prepare the food and comfort. I was a proud man when I invited the first guest into our private dwelling. We seated ourselves and soon fell into lively chat and good humour. We told tales and fantasy myths as if they were our own. Throughout all this time my lady remained in the kitchen and private rooms. I too respected this caution for my lady was still an unknown guest in this uncertain citadel. It was as if she existed only for me. Yet in truth it was I who existed only for her. In all our time together, she had shown me no favours and spoke but few words to me. Still I was not undeterred.

The hired servants fed us two men lavishly with rich food and wine. Yet once again a time came during our merriment when my friend's happiness waned. I soon caught this mood change and asked of my friend's pain.

'Once again I am afflicted with the absence of my beloved,' said the jeweller with a love-stricken tone. I was abhorrent of his witch-like lover and yet felt compelled by the courtesies of hospitality to insist he invite her here. A servant was dispatched immediately with the order, and my friend soon relaxed.

The old hag entered dressed in the jeweller's own finest treasures. From her skin hung the finest gems, yet they could not dress this mutton up as lamb. In polite reverence we drank together. My incredulity mocked me as I watched this pair lather themselves in assiduous kisses. Like craftsmen they worked at each other with great care and attention. Amidst the revelry I drank to their fortune and toasted their happiness. And within this debauchery we hasted towards our own drunken demise.

I awoke with a pounding head. It felt like a bloated pig's bladder that had been kicked around the dirty streets. Throbbing and fragile I sat up to see the room bare. All decorations had been stripped. Only a bundle of sacking remained in one corner. Dragging myself over I pulled aside the sacking…. to my horror! Underneath it lay the blooded bodies of my young jeweller friend and his beloved hag. They had been cut to pieces. In shock I stumbled away, my stomach in knots and near convulsion. What had gone so drastically wrong with my newly ordered world?

I sat dumbfounded against a bare wall. I had checked the house and my beloved was not to be found. Oh, my beloved, do not turn away. Do not cast your face in shadow; I long to be burned by your look.

Then an unknown face appeared and stood near to me. His features were strong; he looked gallant and fierce. Looking down at my crumpled frame he said, 'the young lady is safe, yet she is disappointed that you drink and toast her murderers. She will not speak with you again, yet you may glimpse her if you come to this address.' And he told me to go to a small garden not far from here.

Of course, I wasted no time. I was a man bereft and soulless. There was neither time nor substance to my life now. I was once again a beggar caught between the warring factions of fate. The scarred retina of my mind had been engraved with the demeanour of this once-bloodied Dionysus. I longed for just a look from her. I stole myself quickly into the small enclosed gardens that lay across from the palace. And for the next two days and nights I lay in agony awaiting her. Neither the moon glowed, nor the sun shone for me in those two bitter days. Pungent was my yearning. Huge was my loss. I felt nearer to the abyss than at any other time in my life. All events until now felt meaningless to me as I was torn living in this endlessly painful moment. Finally, she came to a window in the palace that overlooked the gardens. This princess, for now she clearly was, looked over the gardens as if spying some yonder star. She knew that I lay beneath her gaze; trampled and yet no less happy for the occasion.

From my low position I sucked into me the energy of her presence. For she was like a star to me now. And I had once nurtured her beaten soul back to life. For my misfortune I had just as easily let it go. I had been blind to my own actions; steeped in the wine of my misbehaviours and trespass.

From that brief window glimpse I cowered back into my drunken world. I knew I would wither and attain my treasure no more in this life. I had held it and it had slipped through my fingers disguised. I would have to wait until another life for the next chance to try.

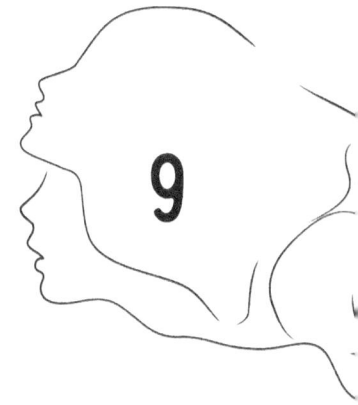

9

'You're becoming a regular,' said the waitress as she re-filled my coffee cup for the second time.

'And I'm drinking too much coffee,' I said.

'Are you sure you are not just drinking to hang around here?'

'Sure, I am.' I smiled.

'Sure you are what? That you're just hanging around or not hanging around?'

'Both.'

'Come on!' she said almost teasingly. First you get a coffee high and tell me you love me; now you answer in riddles.' The waitress walked away from the diner bar shaking her head. I liked the way she had taken to me.

I read the newspaper headlines. Everything had been chaotic after the Event. Chaos was reigning these days as if it were the only energy available. Perhaps it was the only energy that could survive? Yet the newspaper looked old and well-thumbed. I tried to see what date it was, yet the ink blurred into a black ridge…perhaps I needed glasses? To think about it, I had no idea what the date was, or had been, or was to be. Were there any dates in this life? Outside was a constant grey. Streets deserted like ruined landscapes. Here there was sanctuary, a place of retreat from the decay outside. Yet there was something else too. Like an intense familiarity. A thread to some purpose, pulling me towards some remembered place.

'Less and less people come around here nowadays,' the waitress said as she returned to lean upon the counter.

'Why is that?' I asked, both curious and not curious.

'It's the changes. It all started after the Event.' She pulled a grimace like one bitten by a scorpion.

'Why did it have to happen?' I asked blankly. My mind was foggy, misted over as if straining for a lost recollection. Why could I not remember? I glanced again at the newspaper images. Streets of desolation, scavengers amid the broken street signs. I looked down at my own hands. They were calloused and peeling at the fingertips - then blurry. My hands went out of focus as I strained my eyes to see, to concentrate. I was losing myself again; drifting away from something I couldn't hold. I blinked my eyes as the waitress turned her back and walked away.

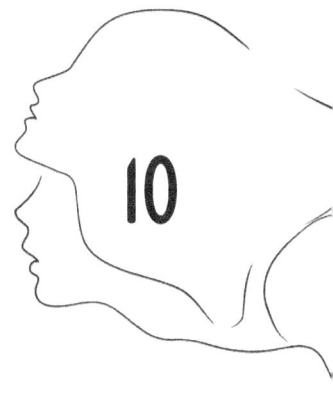

10

King Ahmed Bakht sat back in the bushes after hearing the first dervish speak. Something in the story affected him deeply. He felt his own heart beating with a longing. How at this very moment he would wish to trade places with the young man and to relinquish life for such great passion. He dropped his head into his hands. Weariness tugged at his whole body; he felt heavy as if anchored to the ground. Pangs of some bodily emotion rippled through him. Again, peering from out behind the bush he saw the four dervishes sat in flame-light reverie. Then the second dervish spoke:

"I will relate to you what is known of the most generous king who ever lived. He goes by the name of Reza Arasteh. Reza was so loved by his people that he reigned for decades in his kingdom with no strife or need for force. It was indeed a harmonious reign for the king and his people. Yet such balance by its very nature attracts its opposite. As sure as day and night, Reza's kingdom was coveted when a neighbouring region crowned its new king – Nastah, son of Baztek. No sooner had Nastah ascended to his kingly pedestal he hungered to conquer Reza's humble kingdom. Soon a vast army was assembled that thundered with incredible military might. Word of Nastah's impending power spread fast amongst neighbouring lands.

Fear began to arise amongst the people. A fear that had never before been known so blatantly. It gripped the hearts of many and rendered them feeble and with great panic. The mood changed quickly in the lands of Reza. It soon became apparent that with or without a military invasion, Reza's kingdom had already become blighted by the ravages of a crippling parasite – of fear and defeat. It was in such circumstances that Reza knew only action could prove of worth. Not an equal reaction; nor fateful non-action. But subtlety cloaked in the garments of sincerity.

In wishing to bring no bloodshed to his people Reza stepped down from his throne and disappeared into his lands. He had vanished from the presence of his people; not a trace remained of him, or an explanation given. The oddity of such behaviour (which bewildered some and angered others) was soon spread through neighbouring lands and to the ear of Nastah. With great pride, and mounted upon his most glorious stead, Nastah rode at the head of his mighty army into Reza's lands without a single raised voice in opposition.

Upon arriving at the now vacated palace, Nastah demanded to know the whereabouts of its former king so that he could formally conquer the unfortunate Reza. Yet no answer could be given. Each and all were equally dumbstruck as to what had happened to their once-glorious King Reza. Nastah was furious at such insolence and unkingly behaviour; it was far and beyond his mindset to conceive. In desperation he announced a reward of a thousand gold pieces to anyone who could either deliver to him the personage of King Reza or disclose his secret whereabouts. News of this remarkable offer soon spread throughout the kingdom. It stoked gossip and fuelled interest in the subject of their still-beloved Reza. Each person, day and night, placed upon their lips the name of King Reza. And in their hearts, they also knew that, despite what their minds might whisper, their King Reza had not deserted them.

One day a poor woodcutter, who was a widower, was sitting in the mountains by an open fire with his daughter. Their poverty brought them little to eat, and even less to hope for. As they ate the last of their soup and dates by the fire, the daughter said to her father:
'Father, just think of what we could do with those thousand gold coins; if only we could find our King Reza. It would solve all of our problems and make our life so much better. We could leave this life of poverty behind. Oh, if King Reza were here now, I would turn him over immediately.'
'What are you talking about child?' said the woodcutter alarmed. 'King Reza has been our most glorious father; we can do him no injustice now. Our poverty is our fate and not to be relieved by a king's head on a plate.'
'But father,' protested the daughter, 'is it not right and fair for a king to look after his subjects, such as we?'

At that moment Reza Arasteh, who had been living in a nearby cave and listening to the conversation, stepped forth into the clearing. 'You are right my child,' he said, 'and you are the moment I have been waiting for. Take me to the despot Nastah and claim your reward!'
'No, we cannot do this!' said the woodcutter, shocked at the sight of Reza standing before them.
'This is not up for debate. Take me to Nastah or I shall be forced to walk there myself,' said Reza defiantly.
'Father, look how opportune this moment is,' begged the daughter.

'Surely we must respect the wishes of our king.'

'No, it is so wrong for us to betray the generous nature of our king. It cannot be!' declared the woodcutter in a raised yet fragile voice. Reza, wasting no time, began to walk down the mountainside, with the woodcutter and his daughter running after him. No sooner had they caught up with Reza and stood before him than a patrol of soldiers appeared and immediately recognised the countenance of the old King Reza. They took the whole retinue into custody and dragged them before their new king, Nastah.

Nastah was overjoyed to see his prize captured before him. He clapped his hands in glee and raised his arms heavenward. 'And who has brought before me my captured and cowardly Reza Arasteh?' he announced.

'We did, your honour,' shouted the soldiers in unison; all greedy for their share of a thousand gold pieces.

'Hear it from the mouth of the witness,' spoke forth Reza, 'for none other than this poor woodcutter and his daughter here found me and were on their way to your palace when we met these soldiers on the road. They are the ones who sought me out and who are in just deserve of your gold reward.' On hearing this the old woodcutter stepped forward and with tears in his eyes related the story as it had unfolded. On hearing the story of Reza's generosity King Nastah fell silent. His body became immovable; not a lip trembled. His eyes sank momentarily into the back of his head.

'So, this is the secret of Reza's rule,' said Nastah when he finally spoke. 'A man so loved by his people that he would leave his throne to avoid their bloodshed, only to return to sacrifice his life for their fortune. This is a man I cannot compete with, for his heart far outweighs my courage. I cannot wage war against such a man; such action would disrupt the order of the heavens. Reza deserves to rule his kingdom for its people are ingrained within his very blood and being.'

Saying this, Nastah granted Reza his freedom and returned his kingdom to him. Nastah soon after left the lands of Reza and returned to the throne of his own kingdom; yet not before honouring the woodcutter and his daughter with a thousand gold pieces from his own purse."

'Let this be the story of the generosity of King Reza Arasteh,' said the second dervish.

Ahmed Bakht was transfixed by what he was hearing upon this night. From under the cover of his hiding place his heart pumped to hear such tales. His eyes had become moist at the generosity of Reza Arasteh, and his longing for the ineffable increased. These were no ordinary tales; these were stories which traversed the inner vessels of a being. Ahmed Bakht knew from that moment on that his life would be inexplicably altered.

'Brethren of freedom, my brothers in spirit, these tales spoken so far have touched my being,' spoke the third dervish. 'In fate do we share these stories, for in each tale there is something for every human heart to dwell upon. In words are truths revealed and awaken slumbering souls. In each syllable spoken are mysteries concealed, and their very manner revealed to those with ears to hear. Now let me be humbled by my own tongue. My story begins as thus:'

"There lived in the hills of the Hindu Kush a mighty swordsmith by the name of Shringar. He was a physically powerful man with arms that could swing a plough. By day he crafted the finest swords and by night his gentle voice sang. Built like a mountain he was yet blessed with the soothing song of a hummingbird. Shringar the swordsmith was renowned throughout his village and beyond for his fine skills. Respected amongst his peers and held in awe by those who felt weakened before him. Whenever the voice of Shringar filled the evening air people would gather around his hut to hear his melodious tales. Of all the songs that Shringar sang there was one especially that captured everyone's hearts: The Paradise of Song. In this tale Shringar would sing of a land faraway over the mountain peaks, in an unknown valley beyond, where all mysteries would be revealed. It was a land of fertile soil and plentiful bounty where each heart could find its wish. It was a song that sang of a paradise truly.

Now Shringar had a passionate longing for a young lady of the village, who went by the name of Latika. Shringar adored Latika and his eyes would follow her whenever she passed. And everyone too knew of Shringar's mad longing for Latika. Sometimes they would tease Shringar, mocking his shyness like a gentle stick to beat him with. Now Shringar was not alone in his passion, for he had a rival in love by the name of Hasan. Hasan the warrior sought Latika's heart as madly as did Shringar. It was a rivalry that all knew would bring disharmony in some future form. Some things can never be resolved without inflicting sorrow. This quandary of love was deeply marked by the ominous touch of some future grief.

One evening, as Shringar sang his prized Paradise of Song, Hasan boldly stood up and declared: 'this song is nonsense, no such place exists nor ever will!'

'This is not true,' said Shringar, 'I know this place exists. It exists in a distant valley as well as within all our hearts.'

'No! You trick all of us with your beguiling tales. They are lies, and you make fools of us all,' shouted Hasan to the expectant crowd.

'This is not so!' shouted back Shringar, now angered by Hasan's public accusations. 'I sing the truth, as I have always sung the truth. It is you whose mouth is made wet with lies.'

'Then go to this paradise of song that you sing about,' said Hasan, knowing that he could catch Shringar in a public promise.

'What?' gasped Shringar.

'Go to this valley that you know is so real. If it exists you can go there, and return to tell us all your tale.'

'But I cannot go there!' pleaded Shringar; 'it is not right that we should seek that which is shielded from us.'

'And why is this?' said Hasan, as he baited the crowd.

'Because that is the natural order of things,' replied Shringar.

'Hah! It is your convenient order of things,' retorted Hasan. 'If you do indeed make this journey to your paradise of song, and return to tell your tale, perhaps Latika will consent to marry you?' Everyone's eyes turned upon Latika who until now had sat silently amongst the crowd.

'I will,' said Latika with a nod of assent. This sent the crowd in cheers, and Shringar to despair, for now the issue had been set. As for crafty Hasan, he never expected Shringar to return and so savoured the day he would take Latika's hand in wedlock.

The next day, Shringar packed a modest bundle of nuts, berries, bread, and water, and set out on his voyage for the valley of the paradise of song. He walked over peaks and through mountain passes; slept in caves and waded through streams. For days, then weeks, did Shringar walk, forever fuelled by the promise of his dear Latika. He scavenged for food from the forest floors, and sang his mournful songs to the evening stars. Yet within his heart Shringar knew that the valley of the paradise of song silently awaited his arrival.

Just when the journey seemed almost unbearable did Shringar emerge from a wooded mountain slope to see the valley spread before him. Through the low lying mist Shringar could see villages and lands shrouded by an iridescent beauty. Shringar carefully made his way down into the valley towards the villages below. As he approached he saw people coming from the fields and from the huts to greet him. Yet when they came near Shringar realised that something very strange was happening….

Many months later, Shringar limped back into his village looking like an old man. He went straight into his old hut and closed the door. As soon as news spread of Shringar's arrival people began to gather at the door of Shringar's hut. Finally, Hasan the warrior, Shringar's old rival, appeared at the door and shouted for Shringar to appear. After several minutes a window slowly opened and in it appeared Shringar's wrinkled face. People gasped and could not believe how old and withered he had become.

'Well, Shringar the swordsmith, did you find the valley of the paradise of song?' asked Hasan.

'I did,' replied Shringar.

'So tell us – what did you find?' demanded Hasan, who was now speaking for the crowd.

Shringar looked at everyone with a weariness no-one had ever seen in him before. And with a hopelessness that Shringar himself had never felt before he began to speak: 'I climbed and I climbed. I walked and I walked. Days became weeks, and weeks became months. For what seemed like an endless age I traversed the mountains and valleys where none had set foot before. And when I thought I had lost all hope I came upon the valley of the paradise of song. This valley is exactly like the valley here in which we live. And then I saw the people: those people are not only like us, they are *exactly us*.'

'What!?' asked Hasan confused.

'For every Shringar, every Hasan, every Latika here', said Shringar, 'there is another one of us over there, exactly the same. When we first see such things we think they are reflections of us. Yet it is we who are the reflections of them; it is we who are the likeness mirrored from them,' said Shringar despondently.

Everyone assumed that Shringar had gone mad from his arduous journey. They soon left him alone and did not notice Shringar's retirement from the world. They hardly noticed that Shringar rapidly grew old and died. In the meantime, Hasan married his love Latika and went about their business as memory of Shringar the swordsmith faded. Yet the Paradise of Song never faded in the hearts of those who had heard it from the mouth of Shringar. Soon, all those people who carried the song within their memory also began to lose heart in their lives. They too began to quickly grow old and die. It was as if they knew somewhere deep inside, that something was going to happen to them over which they had no control and from which they had no hope. From this all interest and vitality in life was lost. The terror of the situation had become known within the seat of their souls."

The third dervish stoked the fire with his stick. Turning to the others he continued: 'it is only once every thousand years that this secret is known by man. When the human mind sees it, it is changed forever. When others hear of it, their hearts wither and die out. Such people fear this as the human tragedy for they are blind to its implications. Such is the nature of their ordinary existence. They cannot see the truth that they have more selves than one; more hopes than one; more chances than one – up there within the valley of the paradise of song.'

Ahmed Bakht, as a king disguised, felt his own heart sink like a cold ocean current. And with the swiftness of an icy stream he saw recollections of his life rush past him. Significant moments scattered into non-visible realms. Bakht felt as if infinity was opening up inside of him and creating emptiness. Prestige melted into nothingness. Self-importance wriggled like a wounded beast caught in the throes of death. A sense of waste began to crush Ahmed Bakht as he crouched forlorn amidst the bushes.

Dawn's early light began to slide through the softening dark. A new day was emerging. Quietly, yet with haste, Ahmed Bakht slipped back to his palace unrecognised and once cleaned and refreshed summoned his trusted advisor to him. The king ordered that the four dervishes be brought before him in hospitality, and gave their whereabouts. Soon the vizier returned with the four ragged dervishes who bowed their respectful greetings. In unison they declared 'Our trusted son, may your life be extended.'
'My life has indeed become extended through your presence,' said the king in polite return. 'Now, I ask you to aid my life further by regaling me with your tales,' said the king.
'Our tales are not for this world,' spoke the first dervish.

'We speak only in accordance with time and need,' said the second.

'We have little to say before a king,' said the third.

'We court not the favour of kings but only our freedom,' said the fourth.

Unperturbed, Ahmed leaned forward in conspiratorial posture: 'Friends, last night I was hidden behind a bush and did listen to your fascinating tales. I admit that they shook me to the core. They rattled my very being. Yet only three tales were told; dawn intervened before the fourth could be revealed. Reveal to me now that fourth tale,' said Ahmed in little more than a whisper. The fourth dervish stepped forward and lowered his head.

'Sire, do not think me discourteous. I cannot yet disclose this tale to you; conditions at present do not permit the telling.'

The king leaned back into his throne and looked thoughtful. Those in the king's service expected some severe punishment to follow, for it was unheard of to deny a royal request. They all assumed the king was considering a suitable punishment for each ragged dervish. To everyone's astonishment a smile broke out upon the king's face. 'Perhaps I could myself create the right conditions for the fourth tale. Would you dervishes permit me to tell my own tale?' All four dervishes bowed and opened the floor to the king's words.

King Ahmed Bakht cleared his throat and began to speak.

11

My song is my life. My voice is my blood. My heart's yearning is for love.

'You're back again,' she said, pouring another coffee. 'You just disappeared the other day. Was it something I said?'

I gazed absently. 'I don't remember - what did you say?'

'That's a fine one!' laughed the waitress. 'Now I know you don't listen to me.' The rain was falling hard outside. I looked at my hands; they seemed thinner than usual and more wrinkled. I put the coffee cup to my mouth. The black liquid slipped in yet I tasted nothing but wetness. I felt both weariness and a deep-seated longing comingle like sisters. I felt as if I were patched together and not wholly present. A few other punters hung around the diner. Their faces seemed half-familiar, like extras on a film set wandering through. A faint clammy smell hung in the air; a mixture of bodies, apathy, and drifting time.

'Did you get hit hard?' asked the waitress as she slouched on the counter. Her manner towards me was becoming increasingly casual. I must now be classed as a regular by her.

'Hard by what?' I asked.

'By the Event, of course – what else!' she said, as if it were the most obvious thing.

My mind was blank, intruded only by a nagging lost certainty.

'I don't remember much,' I confessed. It was the truth, even if I was lying.

'Must have got you bad, love,' she replied, with a placid face. Was it something in her that I loved? Why love, was there nothing else? 'It hit us all hard. Riots everywhere; it was pure anarchy. People began to disappear; it happened to the rich ones first. They just left, leaving behind no trace. Then it happened nearly all the time…and to all different people. They just vanished as if they never existed. And then we began to forget about who had left and who were still around. We couldn't even remember our loved ones or friends. Everything just became a blur, a confusion,' she related mournfully. 'This place keeps going as long as it can; as long as there are people coming in. But things are quieter now, and many forget that we still serve coffee. Sometimes, I even forget how to make the coffee!' The waitress smiled as she moved off to serve another customer.

Whatever I had lost it was not coming back. Like a virus, there was a feeling that each one of us had been eaten away from the inside. We had been greedy. We had been exploited. They made us fear; they made us afraid. And we fell like empty phosphorus shells.

We could have made it though. Perhaps there is still a chance. There is always a chance. We only need to remember…

12

'I inherited the throne at a young age, at twenty-five, when my father died,' said Ahmed Bakht. 'I was impetuous and arrogant. I thought that to rule meant that one had to be cruel; that power was a force to wield. Now, I have realised that true power resides in forces outside our control. Further, that we can gain influence with this power if we align our actions to it. We are not in control of our lives, although it may appear that we are. Yet we can direct our actions so that we make a connection with the forces in our lives.' The king paused as if to allow his words to settle. The four dervishes remained impassive with heads bowed. 'Allow me to continue' said the king, 'and I shall explain further.'

"As an eager and youthful king, I was determined to hold power and wealth in the palm of my hand. Riches I amassed through gifts, taxes, and plunder. One of my prized possessions was a ruby that shone as red as the fiery heavens. It was the largest jewel I had ever held between my fingers, and its presence brought me great joy. When dignitaries visited I would often display this ruby with delight and greed. I envisioned that it radiated my power. One day a senior aide spoke in my ear. He said 'Oh great king, trust me when I speak truly to you for I care for your well-being. But this pride you put in your jewel is beneath you and may cause your disgrace. Visitors from afar may return to their lands saying that the king here behaves like a child with his jewels, and puts more faith in objects than he does his rule. Sire, jewels are jewels. In fact I can attest that I have heard of a merchant who places larger rubies around the collar of his dog.'

When I heard this I was raving mad! How dare this aide speak to me in this manner? How dare he suggest that I be upstaged by a dog! I shouted out loud for this man to be executed in my presence. This startled my audience, and one of the dignitaries was bold enough to ask after my insult. So I declared that this rotten man had dared to say a dog had finer rubies on its collar than mine.

'Is your aide a liar by nature?' asked the foreign dignitary.

'No, he is not. He has been loyal in my service until this very day,' I replied truthfully.

'Then could not this report be true?' he asked. 'Would it not be gracious of your lordship to grant a stay of execution until more be known?'

I confess that my anger had begun to subside by this point. My rational mind was once again at the fore of my thinking. So I decreed that my careless advisor be imprisoned in the palace for one year. Upon which time if no truth be found for his remarks he would be executed one year to the day. This was the limit of my generosity in those days. In my role before country and people I felt obliged to exhibit power as a presence; to show knowledge only as a form of power. Ah, if only power were knowledge then life's long routes would be graciously shortened! I was too immature to know that subtle energy is powerful and powerful energy is subtle. The journey we make is one often trod through ignorance. Our destination lives on in our heads whilst we neglect the soft murmurings of the heart. In my stubbornness I subjected my faithful aide to a year of confinement, starved of family to warm him. My hand had fallen over the fate of another man's life. Yet unbeknownst to me, this aide's family had taken the affairs of destiny into their own hands.

The daughter of my imprisoned aide took it upon herself to liberate her grieved father. So no sooner had she received the sorrowful news from her mother than she gathered a few belongings and set off in search of the merchant with the ruby-collared dog. As it was related to me by her very own words, I shall now relate to you. This is her story…

"I was not prepared to let my dear father be executed for I knew he spoke the truth. He always spoke the truth. He was as reliable as the celestial heavens; as selfless as the sun that rises on each morn. He made me the person that I am. I am his heart and his heart beats in me. For him to be incarcerated is like boxing my beating heart. My blood is strangulated at the thought of his punishment. So I throw myself in his service. I am nothing more than his right arm.

Dressed as a young boy I set out on our strongest horse into the world. It was my mission to find the jewelled-dog without delay.

I rode into town after town like a wandering tuneless minstrel. At each town I made my way first to the souks, the market of merchants. I made enquiries yet each response was the same and saddened my heart. Yet I remained determined in my faith. I was fixed in my desire to fulfil my goal.

Finally, in the fourth month of my seeking I came upon a small town that spoke of riches and honour. The streets were lined with majestic houses and overflowing gardens. Here, I felt, lay the answer to my seeking.

Finely robed citizens in the streets greeted me with words of welcome and kind gestures. Immediately I felt at ease in this strange yet mesmerizing place. Here, nothing felt out of place; and yet it was a place that seemed to exist within its own enchanting perimeters. As I continued to pass through the streets with my horse I felt a rising happiness and contentment invade my being. If not a place of magical enchantment then it was certainly a town of cheerfulness that fed its citizens with fine energy and exuberance.

I stopped at a teahouse to take a little rest and gather my thoughts.
'Welcome honoured guest,' said a man seated on a table near to mine. 'You are a stranger to this town. It is my wish to offer you help and assistance - how may I best serve you?'
I looked at the man with wide eyes, startled by such generosity and gentle approach.
'You are right,' I said. 'I am a stranger to these parts. And it is my quest to find the owner of a dog whose collar is fitted with the finest rubies.' The man looked at me kindly yet seemed to pierce the cornea of my eyes. Could he see that I was a girl? Was my sex visible to eyes that penetrate beyond the obvious?
'Of course,' he replied with a gentle and reassuring smile. 'The person that you seek is Salik the Jeweller. You will find him within the passageway of jewellers within the covered market. Please, it would be my honour to show you the way.'
'Oh, thank you,' I replied somewhat hastily. 'Yet there is no need to

show me. Your kindness has been already great.'

'No!' insisted the man, his middle-aged eyes widening in plea. 'I must take you; I would be failing in my duty if I did not.'

'Fail in your duty? What do you mean? I am a stranger to you and thus you owe me no duty,' I said, wishing to appease the man and place him under no further obligation.

'Ah, yes, you are indeed a stranger. And so you do not know of the ways of our town. The chief of our town is a lady whose fairness and generosity is beyond compare. The chief characteristic of our town is hospitality. As long as each citizen practices hospitality to the limits of their ability, our town will continue to prosper in good fortune. So, you see, we cannot be any other than hospitable to strangers such as yourself.'

'Oh, I see,' I said. It was incredible to hear of such a thing; yet wonderful it was. Not wanting to appear rude or disrespectful I agreed to the man helping me.

I could not even dissuade the middle-aged gentleman from paying for my tea. He was insistent that all my needs should be met in the generous spirit of the town. The gentleman – a well-dressed merchant of fine cloth – led me through the alleyways of the town towards the large covered market. All citizens that passed us nodded their heads and addressed us in daily greetings. I felt ashamed at my initial suspicions and mistrust. I had never experienced such generous and well-mannered behaviour before. Soon we had arrived at the jeweller's quarter of the bazaar and my host pointed me to a small shop tucked away in one corner.

'There you will find the owner of the ruby-collared dog. May you go in peace and find your heart's destination,' said my host the cloth merchant.

'Thank you,' I replied hesitantly. 'Yet I cannot truly say what my heart's desire is.'

'No-one passes through here without a desire in their heart. This town cannot be found by the heartless or those with no destiny. Your reason shall be revealed.' And with this the cloth merchant politely bowed and disappeared into the market alleyways.

I now stood before the finely decorated shop. In its window could be seen jewelled arrangements of fine gems. There was a precision in these arrangements that spoke of delicacy and empathy. Whoever was the owner of the shop was clearly a person of sensitivity to beauty and art. Despite my timidity at entering the shop my boldness of mission activated me. I stepped forward and entered into a cave of treasure. Adorning the sides of the shop were showcases of jewelled symmetry far beyond anything I had seen before. There was a geometry to the shop that emanated harmony and tranquillity. Here things felt ordered and in alignment. Objects seemed to display a relationship to their environment and welcomed the human eye. The displays of wealth showed a softness and from this a warmth radiated into my heart. I was stunned at such natural order.

'Be seated, honoured guest,' came a soft-spoken voice from the corner of the room. I turned to see a young man dressed in a simple tunic of white cloth. His skin was smooth and hairless, and his eyes sparkled with a blue-grey kindness. I was immediately struck by his assured presence. He appeared to be in his early twenties and yet radiated a graceful serenity.

'Sir,' I said, 'I am not here to be a customer. I apologise for this yet I wish to meet with Salik the Jeweller.'

'The person you seek is me,' answered the young man. 'And there is no need for apologies. You are welcome here whether you wish to purchase, feast your eyes for a moment, or to engage me in conversation. Your presence is an honour, and my wish is to serve. Please, be seated and tell me of your travels.'

I sat down on the cushions offered and rather than attempting to spin a fantastical story I instead blurted out, 'I need to know if you have a dog with a ruby collar!' My face immediately blossomed into a ruby colour of its own, so ashamed was I. Aware of this rudeness I again opened my mouth to apologise. Salik held up his hand to stop me before I could embarrass myself further with a web of words.

'A young boy who shows the same curiosity as myself,' said Salik with a warming smile.

'I apologise sir for my sudden rudeness,' I said with genuine regret. 'Yet I have a need for this question. It is urgent that I find this dog, I...I,' I began to stutter - how to tell the tale of my father's imprisonment? My journey dressed as a young boy?

'Any need which is great enough shall find its source,' said Salik. And with this he pursed his lips together and out from his softly-rounded mouth emanated a melodic whistle. In an instant a finely-groomed white dog appeared, walking briskly yet elegantly into the room. A noble beast, graceful and yet bearing a familiar friendliness. I immediately warmed to this dignified creature. Yet my eyes were drawn to a dazzling collar of magnificent rubies attached to its neck. A treasure never even seen upon the necks of princesses.

'Let me present to you my dear companion, Nafisa,' said Salik as the dog sat by his side. The dog – Nafisa - then tilted her head towards me as would an old acquaintance. I smiled, and Nafisa stepped towards me and nudged my hand. She then came even closer, to my sudden anxiety, and rubbed her nose softly against my neck. Then, with a flick of her eyes, returned to her seated place beside the cushion of Salik. Nafisa, in an almost human gesture, turned her neck and nuzzled against Salik's ear, as if in a whisper. A bell was rung and Salik ordered tea for us both.

'No doubt you have a story to tell me,' began Salik. 'For without a story you would not be here now in this search for my Nafisa. Yet before you reveal to me the story you carry within you, I first ask that you listen to the story that I carry.'
I nodded my assent. 'Of course, it would be my honour.'
'Very well then,' smiled Salik. 'It would be a pleasure also to relate the story of myself to such a charming guest.' Salik began to pour from a finely engraved silver samovar.

'It began when I too was a young man....

13

I didn't feel the cold. In fact, I can't remember feeling anything; warmth or chill stayed away from my senses. Perhaps they were crouching in some shelter under my skin. There was a darkened blue haziness outside that sang past the café window in a blur. I was here again – at a place that existed somewhere within – and after – what was being called the Event. And the faces of those that lived looked worn and solemn.

This could not be the café of my first filigree wanderings…where had I drifted to? What threshold had I crossed to be here? Memory…. memory… wake up you sleeping beast.

I looked up to see her staring at me. We locked looks like two carnivores, and there was a glimpse.
'You still keep coming back with a pocketful of nothing!' said the waitress. She was blocking my view of the blank wall ahead.
'What should I have in my pockets - a handful of diamonds?' I replied, trying to raise a smile.
'So, you offer me dust instead of diamonds?' she asked.
I shook my head.
'No, I offer you a deep pool where there's no memory.'

'And is this where you live – in your cold deep pool?'

'I didn't say it was cold,' I replied, looking at the small scar on her left ear. It could have been dirt.

'Would you like to know where I live?' the waitress said, her head tilted slightly.

'Maybe I would.' The coffee cup was refilled.

I don't remember the doors swinging behind me. I followed the waitress out onto the street. There was a smell in the dark hazy evening that hung like sour cherry. We walked by the light of the half-hidden moon. We passed shuffling bodies as if they had stepped out of the wasteland; heads down and bowed. Objects slowly moved by as if time had stepped down to an awkward rhythm. I remembered the absence of sound. It was as if we were all caught in some vacuum or a viscous membrane of time. Pavements turned into stairs as we left the street. We climbed steps of stone as if ascending a deserted ziggurat.

A knock at a door; a face peering through a thin slice of space. We entered into a room where other figures sat huddled. I think I counted six, though I'm not certain. Some sat in silence; others were leaning close as if whispering. They nodded to me as the waitress said some words. I was looking at a picture on the far wall. It looked like a wheat field; golden stalks like a window onto another world. The yellowed intrusion was like a sun peering in.

'We are all family,' said the waitress as she touched my elbow. We moved through a hallway and into another room. It was sparse; a mattress sprawled on the floor; a table and one chair against a wall. Odd items littered the table as if left like a lost game of chess. I sat on the mattress. I was alone in the room. This was not my room.

Nor was it the café. I was losing my memory. In this place it was hard to focus on anything, as if every passing moment stole yet another memory from me. Here was a place for losing time; for losing oneself. I could not remember why I was here.

The waitress returned with a bowl that she placed in my hands. The contents tasted warm and good, like boned water.

'Why did you stay here after the Event?' the waitress asked as she sat down beside me.
'What do you mean?' I could not understand what she was asking.
'Most people left the city. They packed what they could and walked out into the country. Everyone thought it would be better there - and safer. But there were many who stayed. We wanted to be together. It's stronger that way. It was difficult at first, but we got by. It's no good to be alone. Nobody wants to be alone.' The waitress stroked my hair and drew my face towards her. I felt a cold warmth as our cheeks touched. My eyes became heavy. A draining weariness tugged on my body like a damp overcoat.

14

"As a young boy I lived with my parents in a region beyond this valley. It was a region where those who visit rarely remain, and from where few ever leave. Life there was strict and governed by harsh rules. We all obeyed the rules without thinking. Our blind adherence to the laws became our natures. It was all because of our King. It was he whose edicts were so strict that to live we all became bound under his laws. It is hard to remember now how constrictive those days were.

I was born in the city of Acacia and lived with my parents in the merchant quarter. My father was a trader of gems and I his apprentice and courier. My boyhood was passed in pleasant pursuits and practical learning. It was a happy childhood. I was poised to become a partner in my father's business. Yet all this changed when I first glimpsed Kamalina.

The King of Acacia had a beautiful daughter by the name of Kamalina. And not only was she so beautiful but also intelligent and wise. At first she was adored by all of Acacia but then the King, in fear or jealousy, forbade her very name. No longer could we place the name of Kamalina upon our tongue. No-one, except the princess's closest aides, could speak to her directly. The King even forbade people to speak of her, in public or in private, and we were threatened with even the thought of her. In a very short time, the people of Acacia feared the name of Kamalina – the punishment was too great.

Yet one day I, Salik, was walking through a forest near to the edge of our city. I was partly daydreaming, partly admiring the intelligence of Nature and her world when… when I spied…no, not spied… it was pure fate. I saw the beauty that is Kamalina walking with her lady servants near a stream. As she was bending down to pluck a flower from the bank of the stream, our eyes met. I was transfixed. At first I felt a shudder of fear at the thought of this transgression. Yet this quickly passed, and I was left with an overwhelming love. It was like a physical rapture and my body shook. In this state I withdrew from that spot, and dazed I staggered back home. My mind was reeling; my heart jumping around like a wild tiger in a flesh prison. My stomach ached and I could not swallow food.

After two days of this insatiable heart-fever my parents forced me to confess the source of my dis-ease. On hearing of my love for Kamalina my parents were shocked and frightened. They admonished me never to think of this incident again. The princess, they said, was far beyond my reach. Not only that, but if the King found out about my feelings for his daughter I would be imprisoned - at best! My parents, naturally, were worried over my safety and well-being; and no doubt theirs as well. Yet how could I forgo such a crushing fate of love? How could I neglect the feelings roused within my very depths? I was possessed with torrents of meaningfulness. Everything in my life now had meaning – and this meaning was called Kamalina.

Each day I would return to the forest in the hope of being blessed with another sight of my Kamalina. And each day I returned from my search unfulfilled. Yet I never, for a moment, lost my sense of meaning. My only loss was my interest and attention to my work. My father saw my passion for his work wane. In my life there was only one gem now – prized above all others and yet priceless. Yet each is delivered according to the heart.

Unbeknownst to me the princess Kamalina had also fallen in love with me from our first sighting. And in secret she had called her most trusted aide and confided her passion. A plan was devised. This aide was to disguise herself as a pedlar and in visiting each house was to find me. This lady played her part well, and after many visits amongst the houses of our city she one day arrived at our door. Upon recognising me she whispered

'Young man, the princess Kamalina loves you too. And now you must go to her and declare your intent. Everything now rests with you. Do you not know the princess is more precious than the moon?'

Oh, sun of suns, she is more precious than the stars that guide us. And upon this day I was thankful to the star that was indeed guiding our treasured fates. And I promised there and then to make my way to Kamalina. I told this lady to declare my intent to the princess.

In a state of exuberance I packed a bag and left the house almost immediately. I intended to enter the city and make my way to the palace. Shortly, I arrived at one of the main plazas in the city. Here had gathered a crowd and I pushed forward to see the spectacle.

There was a man strapped to a whipping post and was naked to the waist. He had undergone a most severe whipping. The shards of his flesh hung like ploughed furrows on his back. I was repulsed by this bloody sight and shocked at such treatment. What had the man done to deserve this? I asked the person next to me as to the nature of the man's crime

'This was a foolish man,' the bystander said with disdain. 'This crazy fool went through the streets publicly declaring his love for...' and then in a whisper he said, 'for the princess.'

My heart sank like a wounded soldier. I again felt the fear that pervaded Acacia over the strict rules of the King. Should my love be known then I too would be severely punished. What a fool I was for thinking I could escape the wrath of our King. Who was I, a simple Salik, to court the heart of a royal princess?

I must admit that I was wracked with fear for those few moments. Yet my strength and faith soon returned, as did my determination to seek out my Kamalina. I left the crowd at the plaza and continued through the city towards the palace. In my heart I nurtured the image of Kamalina as she bent to pluck the flower by the stream. Her image flowed with the blood through my veins like ambrosia. My enchantment fuelled me forward and I continued on my way.

Soon I passed near the cloth merchants of the city and witnessed a ruckus in progress. A young man was being tossed out of his shop by the King's guards. And all his fine wares, his rich clothes and embroidered garments, were strewn onto the street. To the poor man's distress the guards were distributing his cloth amongst the bystanders. What a road to ruin! Again, I approached the scene and enquired to one of the guards as to the event.

'This lousy wretch does not deserve to be dressed in such fine cloth. He is a cockroach, a slimy conniving usurper,' said the guard with a twisted mouth of disdain.

'But what has he done for such fate to befall him?' I asked again.

'This stinking rogue did dare compose a poem about the King's daughter, our revered princess. How dare he be so bold and arrogant! A wretch he is, and punished he will be. No worthy merchant of our city of Acacia,' said the guard as he spat upon the luckless man.

I sank back in horror. Again, I had been given a warning against my errors. A second wave of doubt and fear pulsed my body and turned my bones cold. For a moment I could not move. My stone body was rooted to the spot like a temple pillar. But my faith was strong, and soon returned to burgeon my love. With my resolve once again strengthened I picked up my steps towards the King's palace. I walked through many streets of Acacia, passing the familiar and the unknown. I passed parts of the city that I had never known and which filled me with new thoughts and images. I realised that everything in this city was so orderly. All was arranged and moved in a deliberate motion. I had never noticed this strange city rhythm before, so used I was to abiding in and near our merchant neighbourhood. Where once I believed our lives to be fluid and creative, I now sensed a slowness and sober resignation. The people were passive, lacking vigour and vitality. I saw this now; and I saw how my own strength and passion of purpose separated me from the sombre mass. I was grateful for such an insight and for my fate delivering this vision to me. I continued, renewed, along my path to the palace.

As I approached the outskirts of the palace grounds I neared a middle-aged man who was idly gazing at the sky. Perhaps he too was seeking the moon within daylight? So as not to disturb his gentle reverie I widened my path to pass him. After I had taken a few more steps I heard a shout and the sounds of a scuffle. I turned my head to see two more of the King's guards arrest the man, chain him, and carry him away forcefully amid pleads for help. What could have been the poor man's crimes? An old woman whom I had not noticed was tutting beside me.

'Tut, tut - what an idle fool,' said the old woman as if to herself.

'What do you mean?' I asked. 'What was so foolish?'

'It is such a crime to be caught looking up at the skies,' said the old woman with a shake of her head.

I was bemused.

'We all know that it only leads to foolish error. We begin with the sky but one day we will find ourselves looking up towards the turret of the princess. Such a forbidden stray of the eyes and wandering heart,' the woman said with obvious pity. 'Such skies are not for the unworthy eyes of our city folk. We all should be content with what we have on the ground. Not go staring up into some dreamlike fantasy. Tis madness and stupidity!' groaned the women before moving away.

I was speechless. In my shock and despair I dropped my head and stared grimly at the ground beneath my feet. I began to trudge forward as my mind was spinning with new fears and apprehensions. In this manner I walked the next few streets, unaware of the sights I passed. I too now felt the constraints of passivity. I longed for my passion to burst forth again through my arteries like a volcanic rupture.

I was suddenly aroused by a tug on my sleeve and when I raised my face I saw a young fair lady with scorning eyes.

'I am the princess's aid who came to find you,' said the young woman in an accusing tone. 'And now I find you here bumbling through the streets. What are you doing? Why haven't you done as promised and made good on your love to the princess? If you keep delaying she may become disenchanted with you. Why haven't you made any steps?' she said harshly.

'I have,' I pleaded. 'I have made progress.'

'What progress?' she asked.

'Well,' I began, 'I have only told my parents about my love and nobody else. Secondly, I have composed no poems about Kamalina…'

'But why are you going around with your head down?' interrupted the young woman.

'Ah, that's because I am protecting myself by not inadvertently looking up towards any windows or in the direction of the princess,' I replied.

'This is no good,' urged the woman. 'You may still get caught for the crime of trying to seek out the princess's footsteps! Now avail yourself and be true in your steps. Hurry up, your time is running out!' And saying this, the woman passed quickly on as if fearing that others may see her talking to me.

Looking directly ahead of me I continued my journey towards the palace. I could not fail with such piercing longing in my heart. I must seek and find my beautiful love!

Yet I had not gone one more street before I heard from somewhere the sounds of wails and shrieks of grief.

'She is dead! Our beloved daughter has been taken from us all! The beauty of Acacia has died so young,' sobbed a woman's voice.

What!! Has the beloved princess Kamalina suddenly died! No, this cannot be! With a sudden drop in the pit of my stomach I ran towards the house where I had heard the sobs. I banged fiercely upon the door. Why had I been so slow! Has fate cruelly ripped out my heart with blunt talons?

The door to the house was opened by a woman with tear-stained reddened eyes.
'Tell me the princess is not dead! Tell me it isn't so!' I gasped.
'What do you mean by this?' asked the woman with barely repressed sobs. 'Are you mocking our family? Can we not mourn our own dear daughter in peace? Our dear sweet only daughter has died of a fever and you burst upon our house. Away with you!' said the woman as she firmly closed the door in my face.

I was relieved of my grief yet spun into a pit of confusion. Had I lost my mind? Was I slowly losing the intention of my heart's desire? I wandered aimlessly until I came to a small city garden with a fountain. Absently I sat down on one of the benches and stared inattentively into the splashing water. I was lost amidst a terrain of bewilderment. I had not even noticed that there was a man sitting next to me. I probably would never have noticed the man if he had not spoken to me.

'Salik.' The man spoke softly yet firmly. 'You are wasting time. You move around the city like a lost dweller. You look up in fear, you look down in fright. You run after a death that is not for you. And yet you are mangled inside by conflict. You are torn by trying to appease everybody without fulfilling yourself. Do not lose the princess. You must know your road.'

The man turned to look at me and his eyes were like jet stone. His stare did not waver nor was unkind. It was, in a word, direct. I remember the surge of despair that swelled within me and caused me to cry out - 'But what can I do?!'

'You need to take the direct road to go straight to the heart of the issue. Yet this is not easy. Because of what influences the people here, and how they allow themselves to be influenced, you cannot make this choice alone. Come with me.'

The man stood up and began to walk away. I felt a wave of energy depart as the mysterious man moved away from the bench. I noticed how he walked with a smooth and rhythmic gait despite his advancing years. Something within me jolted my body upright and before I could think I was at the heels of this aged sage. We walked together in silence through deserted spaces; time passing unnoticed. In what seemed like a fleeting whisper, we arrived at the palace gates. I had remembered nothing of our walk here as if my legs had taken but two steps.

'Are you afraid of death?' asked the sage as we stood under the grand palace gates. 'Do your fear losing your worldly possessions? Do you fear losing your pride, your reputation? Are you afraid to ask for help and advice?'

'Well,' I hesitated, 'I try to behave as others behave; to be good like them. And I avoid those things which people should not indulge in. This is all I know.'

'You,' replied the sage 'only mimic what *some* people do and what *some* people do not do. And you deem these things to be the actions of all. You are not sufficiently aware of what is a true life.' After saying this, the sage knocked thrice at the palace gates. A face appeared in the door of the gate, looked at the both of us, then opened up. Astonishingly, the gatekeeper gave great reverence to my new friend. Within moments we were ushered into the palace and to the court of the King. Although I was a knot of anxiety within, my trust in the sage conveyed calmness to my body.

The sage walked directly up to the throne of the King, bowed deeply, and extended his hand to present me.
'This is Salik,' said the sage. 'He has lived with his imagination and with his fear, and now he has come here to ask you for the hand of your daughter, the princess Kamalina, in marriage.'
The King peered down at me through arrowhead eyes.
'I am the King and ruler of this city and these lands,' said the King in a deep voice. 'There is danger everywhere in our lives. Death reigns everywhere and covets our every move. Each one of us must die and from this none are exempt - not even a King. In our lives we constantly face the possibility of disapproval and disgrace. Yet those who live in fear; those who fear death; and those who cannot endure disapproval and disgrace are forever their own slaves. And it is these such people that I am forced to rule. Are these people worthy of a princess, a daughter of their ruler?' asked the King.

In this moment I felt fearless. 'If it be your wish, Majesty,' I said in a clear and direct voice, 'to kill me now, then kill me now. If it be your will to disapprove of my desire and ambition, then disgrace me now. Yet I tell you now that I am here to ask for the hand in marriage of the princess Kamalina. It is my will for there to be nothing to stand between us.'''

'And this,' said Salik, 'was how I came to marry the most precious jewel of them all – the princess Kamalina. And who now rules this city with a hand of the upmost generosity, and hospitality for all strangers. This is why you are treated as our most honoured guest.'

Saying this, Salik leaned forward with the samovar to pour me another cup.

15

Lying like a thing unspoken. My weakness of perception traces her outline. My senses are limited here, in this realm where we dwell. The room that holds us like ghostly hostages clothes us as a veil. There exists more than can be penetrated here. These are moments that speak of succulence yet lend little. They offer false refugees to the trembling fingers.

I finger her flesh as if it were gold, or shimming sprays of last sunset. Beguiled and listless, I am forgetful of my very reason to be here. In her body lies a garden of flowers. Under duress from the reality that has deceived us, the garden lies locked away and seldom spoken of. It has been my deception to be here. We have all been deceived in our ways; like children gathered up to play. I know we should lament, be strong against the numbing, yet there is something still that lingers out of reach.

'I have to work later,' she says as she turns to face me in the bed. The one blanket covers her right shoulder where the hair hangs down. I wish I had the feelings to explode. I only felt thwarted, somehow cheated from a sensation that is mine to have.

'Yes, I know.' But still I know it's not enough. So I leave my words hanging as if threaded by a fine web of yesteryear. Shame on me; shame on all we have never had or been. Come to the end place where the vacuum may swallow. I have a love I cannot fathom. Ban the beginning and let us arrive at the end. But we have all been dealt the middle. And here it is like an ocean of gel. And yet we both lie as if two stones of silent gesture.

I watch her dress and I want to know more. What really happened? How did we all get to this? Each word now is as precious as platinum; durable and dense, splintered throughout our train of tongues. When once all nation-tongues waggled we did nothing. We sat back and let the words drip like plutonium darts.

The Event changed everything forever, she had said. The waitress speaks little about those times. Only that they have passed, and now we strain to survive what is left us. Perhaps we crossed a threshold we never knew was there. Or 'they' led us like lemmings to the slaughter-cliff. Deranged bits of partial memory fizzle as half-life images in my mind. There are things you can never take back. Things exist that cannot be retrieved. Like the arrow that has already left the bow. And the final destination sinks in as a waiting target. We were all fools – we are all fools.

There is something about her that rips at me. And it hurts.

16

He was a different man to me now. He still looked like the same handsome and youthful Salik, yet the *feeling* was different. Something had shifted from hearing his tale. I at once felt a comradeship; no, a friendship, with this man Salik. I felt that I could trust him and that there was a new assuredness between us. I then began to feel guilty over the deception I was perpetrating. Here I was, an honoured guest being treated with such generous hospitality, and I was masquerading as a young man. Would Salik have confided his tale in me if he had known I was a girl? The thought suddenly clawed at me like ragged pincers.

'I must confess!' I blurted out to my surprise. 'I feel so ashamed at my behaviour. You have treated me with nothing less than upmost respect and yet I have come before you dressed as a deceiver. I am not whom you think I am. I am not a young man, I am a young woman!' I sobbed. I hung my head in shame, awaiting my chastisement. Yet there was nothing, only silence. When I looked up I was not greeted by an angry face, as I had expected, but instead by a warm and friendly smile. Stunned, I could not speak.

'Of course you are a young girl,' replied Salik after a pause. 'Do you think that outward appearances can distort the inner truth?'

A wry smile crept into the corners of my mouth. Then a small giggle emerged, followed by a spontaneous and unstoppable breath of bellowing laughter. Of course!

'Do not feel foolish,' said Salik after the mirth had died down. 'Your disguise was necessary to bring you here – to the destination of your journey. And now it can be discarded for its usefulness has ceased. You may ride a donkey to the door of the house, but you would not enter the house with the donkey. Time now to use your own two feet.' Salik spoke with a glint in his eyes.

'I too had to learn about outward appearances,' continued Salik. 'Several years after my blessed marriage to Kamalina I was visited by the old sage who had first helped me in my quest. Under his tutelage I first learnt of the outward things: the invocations, the prayers, the music, the garb and robes, the fasting, the charity, the gyrations - the list goes on,' said Salik with a flick of his hand. 'Then when I had learnt of these things the sage asked me if I was complete. No, I said, I still felt far from the Truth. I desire to learn of the Truth I told him. So the sage took me on a journey to meet the Proof of the Age.'

'The Proof of the Age?' I interrupted.

'Yes – and I was directed to the Truth. This understanding was given to me. It was then that I understood what all the outwardness really meant. When I returned once again to the world no-one would listen to me. Or rather, no-one *could* listen to me. The outwardness continues and, as predicted by the Proof of the Age, it will continue until the end of time. So you see, I am able to distinguish between what is outward appearance and what is inner Truth. I knew you before you knew yourself.'

'Can I too learn of this Truth?' I asked even before I had thought of what I was saying.

'It may be possible,' replied Salik, 'yet first we need to deal with your situation. We have to present Nafisa to your King and free your father from his unjust imprisonment.'

After two days of rest and enjoyable conversations I returned to my kingdom accompanied by Salik and his faithful dog Nafisa. On arriving at the royal palace I sent a message to the King informing him of my presence and of the dog. A royal court was set up and it was here that I presented Salik and Nafisa. It was a moment of amazement and trepidation. I was unsure as to his majesty's reaction. Would he be glad to finally see the proof of my father's statement and to know that his trusted aide was truthful? Or would he be enraged to be proven unjust? However, with the calm and assured presence of Salik it seemed that the moment was transcended into a court of humanity.

The King's first question to Salik was direct and he asked what was upon the tongues of all those present, including myself.
Salik smiled softly as he listened to the question.
'The reason for having this priceless ruby collar around my dog's neck is to signify the possibility for man's development,' said Salik as he addressed the entire audience. 'Yet the Truth of what you see is different from what is. The rubies on this collar began life as ordinary stones. Through the power of transmutation they have been transformed into these lustrous gems. Their very nature has been altered by the influence of Truth. This is proof that the nature of man can also be transformed from a stubborn rock to the priceless gem of true worth. Yet this is only possible if man be open to the influences of Truth. Likewise, the reverse is possible – that man may be converted to stone through his own heedlessness.'"

'And this is my story,' said King Ahmed Bakht. 'The tale of how I changed my impetuousness and, I hope, some of my heedlessness! After this my advisor was released and given a full public apology. I also offered to compensate him greatly for his pains, but he refused all offers. I asked him to remain in service to me, and promoted, yet he answered that he had decided to seek different nourishment. He left, with his daughter and wife, to live in the place where Salik resides. I heard that they became his disciples and are now upon their Way. May they be blessed."'

After the telling of King Ahmed Bakht's personal tale the court remained piercingly still. In the midst of the silence the fourth dervish stepped forward and humbly bowed before the King.

'Sire, I feel it is now appropriate for me to relate my tale. It concerns the man who went in search of his fate…'

17

I find myself walking the streets each day. The walls I pass are varying shades of grey. They hang like blank murals. Cracks dominate each vestige of concrete. Nature is slowly pulling back, preparing to depart the urban dustbowl. People still move around. There is activity; carrying bags, boxes, many things. They look like soldier ants scurrying the resources home to queenie.

I make my way to where I know the diner to be. It still hangs on the corner like a burning scar. It is there to tell the world that there are some of us who still exist. I push open the door and enter the hazy din. Faces blur like streaks of damp. Blotted patches of light and shade invade me. I sit at the counter.

'Coffee,' I say to the man behind the counter.

'There is no coffee here,' he replies flatly.

'There is always coffee. This is a diner. I drink coffee here,' I say wearily.

'This used to be a diner. We haven't served coffee here since the Event,' says the man. 'We haven't been a real diner since as long as I can remember.'

'But I have been here with coffee….always,' I stutter.

'There is no always. You have not been here always. I don't recognise your face. There is nothing here for you.'

'Where is she?'

'Where is who?'

'The waitress. The woman that I know.'

'There is no waitress here. And you don't know anybody. How can you?'

The man was right - how could I have lost my remembrance so quickly, as if the waitress had been nothing to me? Something must have changed. There had probably been another shift, and I missed the curve. I didn't sense the greater loss, the fuzziness.

I leave the diner and meander back through the routes I think I know. There is no desperation in me. Yet there is an absence.

I return to the flat passing the boding stairwell. Once inside I nod to the seated few and move on through to the bedroom. I feel tired although I do not know what I have done. There is no energy here. It has been stolen away and denied us, as if living in the world of our own inaction. I am inside the room that was our bedroom. These are not the walls I remember. I have forgotten to remember. I was warned not to forget. Remembering is my way back to the place where I need to arrive. I am forgetting so much now. I feel a longing in my stomach, in the place where I need not to forget. In the belly of my remembering there is a hole where the images flow out like etheric tendrils.

I don't understand what it is I am supposed to be doing. There is something I am seeking, not wishing to forget. Yet my remembrance is hidden in some recess I cannot find. I walk, I stumble, I run; I chase a myriad of dreams like sparkles and sea-horses. I am entranced by some vista only revealed to me in part. I am starved of the whole picture like a well that is drained of water. Do you know what this hunger feels like?

'Why do you call it hunger?' says a female voice. I turn around and see a middle-aged woman standing in the doorway. I do not recognise her; her voice is smooth.

'Is it not hunger?' I reply

'No, it is yearning. It is a deep need to be reunited. Don't worry so much; what you long for will eventually arrive. That which has been missing will return to its place. There is a plan - but you must understand.'

'Understand what?'

'Understand that you are a part of the answer. And you must answer yourself.'

I have to search again. There is a part of me that fears to leave. But I loved. I know I loved. In her there was a seed of love. It sparked a remembrance in me. But I lost the focus…

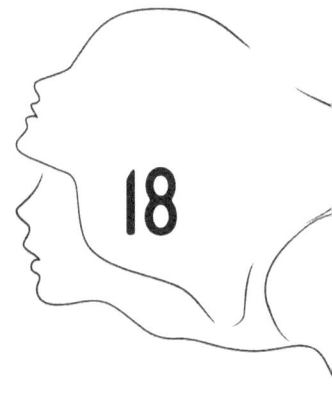

18

"Kemal was a man whom, like many others before and since, decided that he had to make a change in his life. He felt it was necessary that he made an earnest attempt to find his own fate. Hanging around in the waiting room of my life, he thought, will do me no favours. Kemal was anxious to find the meaning that he was sure lay hidden within the core of his existence. He was concerned that in letting things happen to him, in allowing for the circumstances of his life to dictate his experiences, he would miss out on finding his fate. So Kemal believed that he needed to be more active in the ways of his life.

Further, he reasoned, if he worked against his fate he would encounter only suffering, and his life may end-up being only a small and insignificant one. Countless people all over the world lived, according to Kemal, uninteresting and uneventful lives. And this thought caused Kemal great concern, and even bouts of anguish. So in this anxiety Kemal sold his few possessions, closed his house, and set out to become the seeker of his fate.

After Kemal had passed through several towns he decided it was time for a seeker's rest. At the next teahouse Kemal sat down and sipped thoughtfully at his sweet sugary tea. From the corner of his eye he noticed that there was a group of people crowding in the corner of the teahouse. Eyeing this spectacle he soon discovered that the people were listening to a seated dervish who was talking to the crowd. Noticing the extreme coincidence in this event Kemal waited until the small crowd had dispersed and the dervish was alone. He then approached the table and addressed the dervish.

'Man of the Path, I beseech you to hear my request. I am a man who is in search of his fate. I ask you whether you may suggest to me, or give advice, on how I can go about this important quest.'

'This intention is believed to be easier than it is in actual achievement,' replied the dervish. 'It would be better to ask yourself how you might be able to *recognize* your fate for you are a man without preparation.'

'But since it is my fate,' protested Kemal, 'I am sure I will recognize it. Is not one's fate a reflection of oneself? And can I not recognize myself?'

'Seeing oneself externally is not the same as recognizing oneself internally,' said the dervish. 'Each person has many sides to their self, and may not recognize certain signs. Like a mirror the external world can portray a myriad of reflections. Your perceptions require preparation if they are to be able to recognize the signposts for the self,' explained the dervish. Kemal listened with increasing impatience as the dervish went on to talk about the difficulties of recognizing one's fate. Kemal wanted practical advice, not mystical jargon.

'Great sage, all these mystical analogies are indeed useful to one who sits in contemplation, yet I am a man of action. As such, I need to be active to find my fate. If you are travelling may I join you for a while upon your way? Perhaps by being together upon the road I may learn of such practical things as are necessary for me.'

The dervish agreed and shortly the both of them set off together from the teahouse. Soon they arrived at a fork in the road, and beside the crossroads stood a large tree. From this tree could be heard a strong buzzing sound. The dervish told Kemal to put his ear against the trunk of the tree and to tell him what he could hear. Kemal did so and realised that the trunk of the tree must be hollow for he could hear a large number of bees inside.

'The bees must be trapped,' said the dervish. 'If you can break off one of those side branches you will be able to release the bees. It would be a kind gesture to help the trapped bees escape.'

'Oh dervish!' exclaimed Kemal. 'You are not a man of this world. We should not let our intentions be distracted by these trivial matters. We must keep focused on our objective and remain true to ourselves. Let the physical world solve its own dilemmas for we must continue on our search.'

'As is your will,' said the dervish, and the both of them continued walking.

By nightfall the two men found shelter under a canopy of trees and lay down to sleep. In the morning they were awoken by the sound of a donkey passing by with two large jars strapped to its sides. An old man was walking alongside the donkey and when he saw the dervish he greeted him respectfully.

'Good day, Man of the Path,' said the old man.

'Good day to you. And where do you go this day?' enquired the dervish.

'I have good fortune this day,' replied the old man. 'I am going to market to sell this honey which I found and I expect it will fetch me three gold pieces. Yesterday I heard some bees buzzing inside of a tree. So I broke off a branch and let them escape. Inside I found a huge stash of honey. From being a poor man of little means I will now be able to support myself and my family. Blessings to the heavens!' cried the old man and waved his goodbyes.

Kemal sat silent for a few moments before turning to the dervish. 'Maybe I should have gotten to the honey first as you suggested yesterday. But then again, in all likelihood it was a different tree from that which the old man found, and I probably would have been stung anyway. This is not my fate, messing with bees.' The dervish said nothing and again the two travellers went on their way. Later that day they came to a river that was crossed by a wooden bridge. The river stood within a meadow and offered a relaxing spot. As Kemal and the dervish stood gazing at the view a fish poked its head out of the water below and began frantically opening and closing its mouth. 'What is the meaning of this?' asked Kemal.

'The fish looks distressed,' said the dervish. 'Put your hands together with fingers crossing and see if you can hear what the fish is saying.' Kemal followed the dervish's strange request and sure enough he found that he could understand the fish.

'Help me, help me,' cried out the fish.

'What is it you want?' asked Kemal.

'I have swallowed a sharp stone. Please, if you can find some herbs I know that grow on the river bank, and throw them to me, I will be able to bring-up the stone.'

'What is this!' cried Kemal in disbelief. 'You now have me conversing with a fish - what madness are you playing on me? Is this the art of your magic powers?' said Kemal disdainfully. With this, Kemal walked away and the dervish followed without saying a word.

Soon the dervish and Kemal entered a town and sat down in the market square to rest. After only a few minutes a man on a horse came galloping at speed into the square. Dismounting hurriedly the man cried out to the townsfolk:

'A miracle, a miracle!' Soon a crowd had gathered around the man.

'I was crossing a bridge over a river not far from here,' said the man, 'when a fish actually spoke to me! It asked me to throw it some herbs from the riverbank. So I did so in my curiosity, and shortly after the fish threw up a huge diamond. It's flawless and of the highest calibre!'

'How can you be so sure of its quality – maybe it's just a shiny stone?' asked Kemal.

'Oh no, I am a jeweller,' replied the man. 'I know of these things. I am truly wealthy beyond all belief.'

'This is typical of life,' said Kemal to the dervish. 'Fate gives this man more wealth than he could possibly need. And yet I, who am focused with intent upon my own objective path, am denied such things. My dedication has kept me in poverty and forced me to remain in the company of an ineffective dervish. Typical!'

'Oh well,' said the dervish. 'Perhaps it was not the same fish after all. And maybe the man is just lying to gain attention. Let us move on.'

'Yes, indeed, these are my own thoughts exactly,' said Kemal. The two travellers once again went on their way.

The journey continued, and later in the afternoon they both stopped to rest and to eat a little. They sat down beside a rock on which to lean against. Both men realised that a low humming sound was coming from the rock. Puzzled, Kemal put his ear to the rock and found that if he listened carefully he could understand what the humming meant. It was coming from a group of ants who were saying,

'If only we could move this rock, we would be able to move further and extend our kingdom. We need more space. But we are trapped by this heavy substance – if only something could take it away!'

Kemal looked at the dervish with a frown. 'All this animal talk – now the ants want their kingdom extended! I am on my quest to find my fate and all I encounter are trivial requests from the small creatures of the Earth. I cannot possibly waste all my time on these events. After all, there is a natural order and Nature must look after her own. We higher men have the ability to seek our fates, and this is what I intend to do.' The dervish said nothing; and so, after a little food the two men once again continued on their way.

As night drew in, the dervish and Kemal found a dry hedge to sleep under. The following morning they were awoken by the sound of fanfare and much cheering. When they had fully opened their eyes they saw a procession of people passing near to them. There was music, singing, and much joviality. Some of the people were dancing and others were jumping with great joy. As one of them passed, Kemal called out and enquired as to the reason for the carnival.

'Believe it or not,' said one of the dancers, 'one of our shepherds heard a group of ants in distress and lifted a rock to help them. And what did he find? He found a huge treasure of gold pieces. And he's sharing it between the whole village – we are a village renewed! What a miracle!' said the dancer and danced away. As the villagers passed in their ecstatic delight Kemal sat stunned in silence. Now it was the turn of the dervish to speak.

'You are a fool for you have repeatedly failed to do even the simplest of tasks! Not only have you denied yourself the fortune that would have secured your worldly life but you have shown how unprepared you truly are. You could not even provide the simplest of kindly acts as part of your search for your fate. Your obsession to find fate and your personal desires have blinded you and rendered you useless. You have managed the reverse of your intention for you have distanced yourself from your fate by your inability to see what is right beneath your very nose. And above all,' said the dervish, 'you are a fool because despite your pretentions to Truth you have repeatedly neglected my advice and my indications. The signs were there for you to see!'

Kemal became enraged at the dervish's words. He felt that he did not deserve such harsh criticisms – even from a so-called Man of the Path.

'And who are you anyway!' cried out Kemal. 'A self-satisfied wandering mendicant. Ha, anyone can be wise after the event. And if you are so wise, how is it that you could not take advantage of these situations? Why is it that you remain a poor beggar despite these riches you criticize me of - perhaps you can tell me why that is?'

'I can indeed,' replied the dervish. 'I could not benefit myself because I had other things to do. You see – I *am* your fate!' And with this the dervish disappeared; and has never been seen of again - at least not by Kemal.

As for Kemal, he is still looking for his fate, convinced it will return to him for it is his right, after all, to own his own fate. Is it not?"

Saying this, the fourth dervish once again bowed before the King and stepped back to join his three comrades. Four dervishes now stood before King Ahmed Bakht. All tales told.

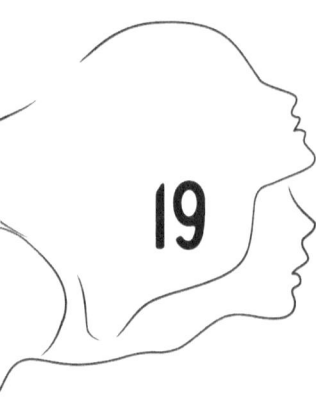

19

I sat on a bench in the open plaza. All around me floated the remnants of litter and written pages from lost books. Knowledge, passion, secrets...juvenile diaries and philosophic treatises mixed with scientific equations and lonely murmurings. All the words that once existed as liquid lines on paper now coalesced into a sea of squid-ink. There was nothing left to capture our memories anymore. Myths collided with historical fact along the rubbish-strewn streets. All distinguishing features erased into a blandness of sameness. Had we done this to ourselves? A fragment of memory lingered in my mind's recess; a memory of some age of diversity. An age of colours...of something...now strung apart and left dangling like a used noose. I realised there was no sun here, just alternate shades of grey.

Several dirty children sat amongst some stones. Their thinned fingers clambered amidst the piles of rubble for assorted shapes and playful things. They were once a link to the past - our past. A past now closed and eroding away. This was what the Event had done to us; to all of us. It had denied us our heritage by closing off the connection to our own presence. The present that now hung over us was erasing our memories and shrinking the space from which we breathed. It had begun with the collective forgetting. All of us, at some point, must have sensed this. A time when, as a species, we forget our wholeness. Our racial memories denied to us, closed off through neglect and ignorance. Surely we must have sensed this moment, this blockage?

Then it began on an individual level. Each one of us lost something in our faces. Now, it is as if there are no faces anymore. No names either. Just a feeling that what still remains waits deep inside to be found again.

The children can no longer be responsible for the future. They are no longer carriers of the message. They are like us: waiting.

I see a woman looking at me from a nearby bench. Under her hands she carelessly caresses the straggly hair of a young baby girl. The woman is biting her lips as she stares. I sense a yearning, as if half her mind is elsewhere and occupied in some attempt at recollection. I remain within her line of vision. Then for an instant, something changes. A quick sudden blur that shimmered over the picture. What was it….? What do you call that thing… that used to be there in all things… yes, I know it… it was a …a…colour…a redness, yes… that's it…

I had seen a sudden redness that wavered where her hair fell over her face.

It must have been an impulse. Yet I stood up and walked over to the bench where she sat. Soon I was standing directly in front of her. She did not move nor acknowledge my presence. I sat down beside her on the bench and looked into the dreamy eyes of the baby girl. Her scrubby face grinned at me like thoughtless innocence.

'We forget that we are invisible,' said the woman without turning her head. 'We do not realize that we are in a world of invisible people.' I remained silent, not knowing if this talk was her own thoughts aloud.

'Our life,' she continued, 'was a drama of the visible and the invisible. Then we forgot completely to be visible. And everything sank away; everything became the invisible. We lost our polarity. We lost the game. I don't know if we'll ever find our way back.'

'The Event?' I asked.

'Yes, the Event. That was the final cut-off. But it had started long before then. People don't care to think about it. It's gone; it has past. Whether it happened at once or gradually…these are idle questions to the people.'

'Do you remember the Event?' I asked. I felt a giddy curiosity rise in my stomach.

'Just things. I see a patchwork of images, colours, and sounds… fragments of lives. They run through my mind but I cannot hold them. Yet I cannot let go of them either. I don't want to let them go…not forever,' she said turning to me. Her face was young and slender, split in the middle by a long and bony nose. Her eyes were piercing yet also misty.

'What do you remember of the Event?' she asked.

I looked back dumbly into her face.

'Nothing,' I said. 'I don't even know if there was an Event. I hear only in what whispers people tell. I wish I knew though.'

'Can you see?' she asked. This time her eyes seemed more focused on me. She was reaching out for something.

'See? I see, yes, I see.' I replied hesitantly.

'No. I mean really seeing. Have you seen the colours?' the woman asked.

Again, I hesitated.

'You mean, like the reds?' I spoke softly. I did not want to be overheard. I began to feel as if we had entered into a forbidden topic.

'Not just the reds. All of them,' the woman replied.

'I see some things,' I confessed. 'I saw reds a moment ago. And I think I saw others when I was in the diner. Yes. I used to go to a diner. There were more colours there. But now I don't see them so much.'

'We must not forget. It is all we have. There are not many memories left. Come with me.'

The woman stood up still cradling the baby girl in her arms. She moved from the bench and walked off, away from the plaza. I stood still for several seconds before trailing behind her. I glanced up at the blanket-cloud sky. Grey, as always…the sameness…severing the sky and the stones. Buildings like bent daggers staggered upwards. Broken glass and debris married themselves amongst cracks and paths.

I quickened my steps.

20

The first dervish stepped forward and turned to face the gathering at the head of the King's court.

'Brothers, Brethren of freedom, my family in spirit,' began the first dervish, 'I now feel I have glimpsed the motive for our gathering together. All tales are told for a reason. Each has its own unique impact. And hearing all of our tales together I have come to understand what lies ahead on the Path for me. We have not witnessed four tales here, but five. And it was the tale of our gracious host, King Ahmed Bakht, which has provided the answer to my own seeking. For I have been seeking the "great one" – the Proof of the Age.'

The three other dervishes listened attentively, as did the King, as the first dervish went on to explain the circumstances of his being here.

'My own great teacher, peace upon his name, spoke to me but once about the Pillar of Wisdom. He said that people in all times have attempted to seek out the Proof of the Age, yet many in their hearts carry petty reasons. For their efforts they gain little advantage for they are not open to the Ways of each Age. It was said by my teacher that by the very existence of the Proof of the Age we each have great opportunity. The greatest of these is that the whole human community, and not just those who 'believe,' continue to exist in physical form because of the life and work of the Proof of the Age. And that this great secret is so astonishing and 'unbelievable' that it is called, by all great teachers, as 'the secret that protects itself by its own implausibility.'

'It is thus my Path that I seek contact with this Proof of the Age. And hearing Salik mention, within the tale of our gracious King Ahmed Bakht, of such a contact has provided me the sign for my next step. I shall depart herewith, take absence of my beloved companions of the road, and seek out this person Salik. I know that this is the journey for which I have been prepared.'

'My brother,' said the second dervish, 'do not be in such haste. There is more here than we have been permitted to perceive. For those very words that you spoke were also spoken to me by my great teacher. I too am seeking the Proof of the Age. Our stories have united us in our seeking. Let us be brothers together on this Path.'

'Journeymen,' said the third dervish stepping forth. 'It appears that there is a blessed intervention in our fortunate gathering - for I too am seeking the Proof of the Age after the very same words from my teacher. This is the reason for my wanderings upon the many roads of yonder years. Let us take this journey together.'

'Band of brothers,' said the fourth dervish, 'do not expect to leave this one behind. Is it not divine that I too should confess to the same reason for my seeking? Yes, my teacher spoke to me of the Proof of the Age and thus began my search. Here we are, united in purpose and intention, strengthening our energies and resolve. Let us not be four but one – one body seeking one goal.'

With a royal blessing the four dervishes departed the kingdom of King Ahmed Bakht. They were never seen of again. Yet rumours soon spread of a small circle of wise elders that existed in the heart of the most generous city ever known. There, it was said, the brotherhood of humanity was kept alive, and the Earth upon her axis.

21

They looked like a bunch of ragged nomads scraping for survival. There were nine of them, a council of the wise, huddled within the station master's office in a disused railway station. The shared rooms were peeling humidity, falling petals of paper climbing down the walls. Yet there was a gesture of nobility, of defiance, within the faces I met. The group consisted of four women, three men, and two children. For my part, I was not yet to be among the counted.

They were, they confessed, earnestly seeking for the Portal.
'The Portal?' I asked.
'Yes,' said the woman from the plaza. Her young child was mingling at her feet as if an eel lost amidst the weeds of a river bed.
'What is the Portal?'
'It is our way back to remembrance. It is our only way of leaving,' the woman replied with a strained look.
'Yes, the Portal,' I mouthed absently as if struck by a vague recollection that hung silently in a hall of masterpieces. The name 'The Portal' struck something in me. As I began to think a little harder, pushing against the cloud of mental apathy, I again saw those flickers of colours that periodically plagued me. Strips of blue clung to the walls of the room, gazing back at my eye's penetration,

then fading into milkweed smudges. Sprinkles of amber nestled in the corners of the cracked windows as if hiding from the onslaught of simulacra. All pairs of eyes were reaching out for me now as if desirous to share in my visions.

'You know about the Portal, don't you?' asked another voice, this time a man's. In this masculine tone I could taste the rusty salt of desperation and the sweat of hope. I hesitated, unsure of what to say at this time. I was not even sure of my own senses, at my ephemeral fragments of recollection. Yet I felt that something, I don't know what, was trying to get through to me. Someone had set the alarm ticking and some last vestige of longing was urging its way through. These were the signs, I told myself, which marked the road for all lost travelers. We are urged on by a planted fragment of the original longing. It remains inside of us as the last marker, its beacon becoming fainter with each passing epoch.

'I know something of it. I have passed through it recently,' I said finally.

'So you know how to get back?!' said my woman friend, clutching at my arm.

'I don't know', I confessed. 'I am losing my remembrance more as time passes. Soon I will have nothing left.'

'Then we must move soon,' said the man's voice.

'I knew we would find a Rememberer,' said the woman to the group. All faces smiled; fingers touched lips as a nearly forgotten remnant of wonder.

'A Rememberer?' I asked softly, my eyes glazing over.

'Yes,' said the woman, 'a person who is new to this realm and who still carries within them some of their original memories.'

'We are always on the look-out for new ones. You still see colours sometimes, don't you?' asked the man.

'I think they are colours. They come into my sight suddenly like invasive flares,' I replied.

'What are they like?' asked a different voice.

'Strange,' I said. 'They feel alien, like they don't belong.'

'We don't belong!' said a man's voice slightly raised.

'What are you doing here?' I asked the group that was now crowding around me.

'We got lost,' said the woman from the plaza. 'We all got lost. We need to move on, not be stuck here in this…this…' The woman hesitated, then dropped her head knowing she was lost for any words to suffice. There appeared to be no words for where we were.

'Is this not real?' I finally asked.

'Real as any shadows ever are - or ever will be,' said the first man's voice.

I bent down to look at the young baby girl. Her cheeks puffed like two fleshy hillocks. Her nose a dimple, a squiggliest snout of sweet skin. I brushed her cheek as she smiled.

'I will try,' I said.

That evening our band of 'Portal-Seekers,' as I had termed them, camped down together, huddled in twos and threes. There was little talk, only the faint hums of whispers sent back and forth between near mouths. The air was odourless and imperceptibly passed our lips. I could not even be sure there was any air, or that we had the need to breath.

'Are you hungry?' I asked the woman from the plaza as she lay her head across my stomach.

'No. We are never hungry. There is no hunger anymore. This need soon leaves you after you have been here awhile.'

'Oh…'

'But it is good you still have the feeling. It means you are still fresh,' she said.

'Fresh?' I did not feel fresh. If anything, I felt like a dusty corner of some abandoned playroom.

'You still hold some of the energies from before. You must remember…before it becomes too late for you.'

'It feels like I am already losing all that I had,' I said despondently.

'What do you mean?'

'All I remember when I came here was the waitress in the café.' My mind was thrashing against a rising tide to return to the image of the waitress…of the love I knew I had yet could not fathom.

'Is this your first memory – the café?' she asked, pressing her fingers into my belly. I could only just discern her touch; like vesicles of torn desire. I squeezed my mind hard to recall those moments…now seemingly far away as if belonging to an ancestor's photo album. I could no longer be sure that these fractal memories were mine, or whether implanted by the vacuous eyes of passing strangers.

'Yes, it all began in the café. There was nothing before. I loved her in the café…and I drank coffee to see her…' my voice trailing off.

I slept until the young child awoke me by pulling on my hair. She looked older. For a brief moment we stared at one another like silent witnesses. She had more answers than I could ever confess to.

Then something sparked the engine of memory deep within the core of my cells…

22

The days passed in troubled thought for King Ahmed Bakht. Since that fateful day he had first openly told the tale of Salik and his jewelled dog he could not rest in peace. Why had he not thought more about this story in all these years? He had let it sit, dormant and quiet, at the back of his skull. Like a hibernating creature it had rested out of vision of his senses. Now he recalled the words that Salik had spoken – how the transformed rubies were proof that the nature of man could be transformed from its lowly state into a priceless gem of true worth. King Ahmed Bakht ran all the words through his head, sweating when he came to the part where Salik had said that the reverse was also possible: that man may be converted to stone through his own heedlessness…

King Ahmed Bakht berated himself in forceful curses over such negligence. Yet a part of him realised that he had served as a carrier for the tale that had been dutifully delivered to the four dervishes. Yet what had been repaid in kind, if anything? Was there a sign smuggled through the tales that he had missed?

Ever since the departure of the four dervishes, King Ahmed Bakht had been in abject bewilderment. He acted like a man with no history;

a person of no presence. Out of time and drifting between spaces. There was no place that the King could find to ground himself. Weightless, denied of gravity, a body floating in the neutrality of indecision. Such directionless momentum grated against the King and tore at his soul.

In such a state, King Ahmed Bakht refused all royal duties and retired to his private quarters once again. This time, instead of delving into deep despair, the King sank into worrying contemplation. No royal vizier or seductive call could bring him out of his walled cocoon. Not until, that is, King Ahmed Bakht had his dream…

…standing by a river, the green swell of the riverbank grass wrestling with the passing breeze… King Ahmed Bakht sees himself dressed in his royal robes, gazing into the multiple rivulets of water rushing by. He turns when he senses another figure by his side. The figure that stands beside him is that of a man dressed all in green. His expression is noble and his gaze penetrating.

'Rip off your weighty robes and unmask yourself,' says the Green Man. King Ahmed Bakht does so and stands naked before the water, before the grass, before the still air, before all…

'You are not King Ahmed Bakht – you are now Ahmed Bakht. Jump into the river and follow your fate,' says the Green Man. Ahmed Bakht does so – he jumps into the river without knowing why, only knowing that he must. He is compelled. He feels the compulsion, and complies with the force tugging at him.

Under the surface he slips, pulled fast with the flowing energies of the water. His arms are stretching for support, for something to cling to. Flailing, thrashing, Ahmed Bakht is dragged, gasping…breaking through to air…lungs straining, heaving for breath…for refill, for the moisture of oxygen to inflate…the river carries him along like an overboard creature; shell-less and vulnerable, fleshy and spongy against the pinnacles of cold ice water than prick his soft skin…

…then hauled upwards; yanked by tight lattice tentacles of rope that bring him onto a rocking wooden vessel. Ahmed Bakht looks up through weeping eyes to see the face that gazes down at him.

'You fool,' said the fisherman, 'what do you think you were doing in the river? And naked as a babe as well! You silly man – here, dry yourself.' The fisherman covers Ahmed Bakht and takes him back to his small cottage where he feeds him some warming fish soup. Ahmed Bakht watches all of this dispassionately as if unable to participate. He is rendered both as observer and main protagonist. Ahmed Bakht feels lifeless and yet strangely human too.

The next few days pass genially; the fisherman takes care of Ahmed Bakht, feeds, clothes, and shelters him. In return, Ahmed Bakht helps the fisherman to read his books and they speak about science and subjects that fascinate the fisherman. It soon seems to Ahmed Bakht that weeks have passed. Then one night when he is sleeping the Green Man once again appears, at the foot of Ahmed Bakht's bed. Sensing a presence, Ahmed Bakht opens his eyes, sees the noble figure, and understands that once again there will be change.

'Leave your bed this very instant. Leave this hut and keep walking until you find that you will be provided for,' says the Green Man. Hypnotically, Ahmed Bakht dresses in his sparse fisherman's clothes and leaves the cottage. His path is outlined by the hazy rays of the moon as they splash upon the delicate outline of Nature. After some time Ahmed Bakht feels the warmth of dawn serenade his face.

Soon a farmer, herding a flock of sheep, passes along the road. On glancing the ragged figure of Ahmed Bakht he calls out: 'Good fellow, are you looking for work? I could use a good farm-hand for the year ahead.' Ahmed Bakht, realising that he could be provided for by this opportunity, readily accepts and goes with the farmer. For the next few months the farmer shows Ahmed Bakht how to herd the flocks, feed the animals, and clean out the sheds. Ahmed Bakht works hard and begins to take pride in his accomplishments. The skin on his hands hardens and his face becomes weathered by the work outdoors. And once again, Ahmed Bakht feels the non-presence of time pass; with himself as both an observer and the main protagonist. Then one afternoon, as he was herding the sheep to new pastures, the figure of the Green Man appeared beside him. 'Leave what you are doing now and keep walking until you reach the nearest town. Here you will establish yourself as a trader.'
Ahmed Bakht again followed the command of the Green Man with unquestioning obedience. After some indefinable time, Ahmed Bakht arrived at the outskirts of a town. He soon found the local bazaar and, after enquiring, took up work as an assistant to a wealthy trader. Again, time passed in imperceptible blocks of ages. Ahmed Bakht worked, learned, experienced, until he finally became a noted trader himself. And at this work he became successful, earning good money and reputation. Until one day, seated at the rear of his shop checking stock, the Green Man appeared before him.
'Leave this place. Walk away now, give all your money to me, and find a city that is a day's walk South-East of here. In this city you will apprentice yourself to a baker.'

Leaving all behind, Ahmed Bakht set out once again in pursuit of a given destination. Arriving at the city he made his way to the street of the bakers and inquired for work. He was given the job of rising early each morning and lighting the fires of the oven. Ahmed Bakht worked hard and without complaint. And although Ahmed Bakht occupied a lowly position people soon began to realise that this solitary baker's assistant was displaying features of illumination. Before long Ahmed Bakht would receive visitors in the dark hours of the morning as he arrived to light the oven fires. They came for council, for advice to heal the sick, for blessings, and all manner of spiritual need. And Ahmed Bakht, without knowing why, found he had direct access to realms of knowledge usually preserved for the Elect.

The rich, powerful, religious, and even royal, came to the bakery to solicit the favours of Ahmed Bakht. And people wanted to know the secret to his wisdom. What was his path to illumination? What was his life story?

'I jumped into a river naked,' said Ahmed Bakht. 'Then I stayed with a fisherman for a while. After that, I left and become a farmhand for some years, herding sheep and cleaning sheds. Then one night I walked out of this and became a trader. After making some money, I gave it all away and came here to be a baker's assistant. This is where I am now.' The people stared at Ahmed Bakht with numb faces; they didn't know whether to believe him or whether it was a test of some kind…

King Ahmed Bakht jumped up suddenly from his bed, his eyes shot wide open, his heart pounding madly against his sweating chest. It had been a dream - yet how so vivid! It had felt like a lifetime... countless years of toil and wandering... he had felt vulnerable, weak, helpless, old; then strong, humble, and wise...the whole vault of human emotions had ran through him like an ecstatic jolt of lightening...

King Ahmed Bakht got up from his bed and went to the wash bowl to wash his face with water. On drying himself with a cloth, he turned to see a figure standing beside his bed. The figure was dressed head to foot in green clothes. King Ahmed Bakht jumped back in shock, unable to utter a sound.

'King Ahmed Bakht,' said the Green Man; 'thou art a King in this realm, yet this is the world of lesser reality. The *invisible world* operates at all times, in all places, and interpenetrates this realm of the lesser. What often passes in this world of yours as inexplicable are frequently the workings of this intervention. Yet people do not recognise it as so because they believe only in the "real" of the senses, the "real" of the secondary. Yet people rarely understand the true cause of events. Only when a person opens their heart to the possibility that another realm penetrates into the affairs of ordinary life can such experiences be available to them. Do not be meagre in your life. Do not be governed by your fears, nor ruled by the shadows of what can be.'

And saying this, the Green Man disappeared from the King's vision. King Ahmed Bakht felt a citadel of relief exude from his stricken body. The portal had been opened, and King Ahmed Bakht knew, for the first time, that the door had never truly been locked.

23

There were no animals. Only now did I realize their absence. Had there been animals before – birds, dogs, flies – but that I had not noticed them? Or perhaps I had noticed them at the time but have now forgotten? Yet now, as I stand on the platform of the old train station, looking out across the broken remnants of rails, I recognise the absence. I want to say that I feel it too; but I don't know that I do. I don't know what it is to *feel* the absence of animals. Perhaps it's not just the animals…perhaps I just don't *feel anything* anymore…

No – this is not true. I feel something for the waitress; I still yearn for the *feeling* I had when I was in the café with her. I can still recall the taste of that…what to call it – longing? Yes, that *longing* that I experienced when in her presence. The waitress drew it out of me with a hooked line. She did nothing; didn't have to do…it was there. A reminder, seeded in me…planted perhaps? A beacon…a signal to return?

I look out over the tracks…into the greying distance…flattened lands reach into far spaces like mummified skin…preserved, acrid, defiant, and unwelcoming…

…is this a place of our own creation? The result of a collective amnesia, an endemic somnambulism?

If this was the price we paid - the so-called 'Event' - then I never want to forget again.

I walk back through the station and into the station master's office. I see the group of nine milling there, trying to remember their sense of expectancy. They look up at me, then I see them squinting as if dredging up into their cerebral moors the reason for my being here.

'I will be back soon,' I say, and step out from the office and into the street. I have the recollection that this used to be a habitual pattern; of "stepping out"…to get some "fresh air." So I make the motions and inhale deeply into my lungs. But I cannot be sure if anything went in, or if anything comes out when I exhale. How can we know there is this thing called air if we only have life or death to tell us?

I see a broken bicycle lying at the side of the road. Its metal is mangled and twisted into death-throes. It takes on several images at once, like a flickering screen; now a robotic skeleton…now a warped instrument of science…now a garbled instrument of war…

Further down the street I see the rotting walls of a church with an empty bell tower preaching on its peak…preaching to the absent… absently I open the stiff wooden door and enter. Inside, the sanctuary has clearly been desecrated. What lies left is a corrupted space - defiled and dirtied. Stains on the walls mark where the icons once proudly peered down to the humble. Iron hooks rust as gnarled fingers absent of touch. Disarrayed pews stretch out in odd alignments before the pulpit. These dead lumber-soldiers held the bodies of the subservient; they held the weight of those bent in prayer. And now they lay as lost coffins to a neglected edifice.

I sit on one of the pews and close my eyes. I listen; hoping to hear for something. Anything other than silence. Yet I am left wanting.

I open my eyes to see a figure seated to my left, at the far end of the pew. She is old, greying hair tied in a careful bun. She wears a black shawl over her shoulders; she is dressed in the garb of one in mourning. I should be shocked at this unexpected appearance; a sudden renewal of life in a place dwelling in absence. Yet there is no shock, only passive curiosity. The old lady turns to me. My eyes widen and my heart thumps into my throat – her eyes are deepest blue. They radiate azure; deep in meaning and…and something else. Yes, I recognise it now – they radiate remembrance.

'You should not be here,' says the old lady. Her voice relays firmness and control; and also sympathy. I say nothing, only stare.
'This place is not for you. Go back. Do not wander in this place; too long here and you will stay. This is a place of quarantine. There are barriers here against the rise of mind. Take your leave now. You know the way out. Follow the last of your longing.' The old lady gets up from the pew with measured grace, and leaves. A part of me understands her words.

I leave the church and head back to the station. Once inside I find the group of nine. They are still mingling like a hypnotic mass, indecisive and uncertain.

'We are going to the Portal now,' I say. 'Follow me.'

24

King Ahmed Bakht left his private quarters a different person. Gone was the fatigue of indecision that had plagued him like a viral infection for so many days. Now each morning offered promise: a sign of renewal and regeneration. In a world of fluidity, King Ahmed Bakht knew that nothing was fixed.

A great celebration was held in the city. Three days of public holiday were declared and a grand street fiesta planned. Artists and musicians came from surrounding areas and each district organized its own festivities. King Ahmed Bakht gave generously to the people; everything was paid for from the royal coffers. No expense was spared. There was much rejoicing and contagious happiness. People celebrated their families, their good fortune, their futures – and their hopes.

And King Ahmed Bakht celebrated his freedom. To be generous without desire for reward is a hard thing to achieve. Yet King Ahmed Bakht succeeded in this endeavour. At this moment, the last thing he wished for was any form of adulation.

It was a celebration that would stimulate each citizen to examine their own lives; their priorities, behaviour, goals and intentions. It was a celebration for focus.

Energy spread through the city like the sun's rays and each and every corner was warmed by it. Every place was touched and no place forgotten. People felt that they had a purpose – a meaning to their lives. And in this, nothing would ever be the same again.

And after the celebration, when the city had returned to its activity, there remained a renewed vigour in everything. Purposefulness, once tasted, is hard to let go of.

King Ahmed Bakht convened his royal council and divested his ruling powers amongst his most capable aides. Then he abdicated, packed a small bag, changed into regular attire, and walked calmly out of his royal residence and into the streets. And far away.

King Ahmed Bakht felt nearly complete. The rest was in his hands.

25

The sun of the summer equinox seeped through the windows of the caravanserai as Babu finished telling his night's tale. He had indeed proven himself to be a Master Storyteller. Bathed in the dawn's early light I felt a different person. I was left shaken; carved out, hollowed, and washed clean.

The ruddy figure of Babu sat serene and calm as people bustled about the now active room. Hands dropped coins before him as people made their leave. We had all been brethren for the night, a group of brothers banded together for the power of tales. And now we each made our separate way into our lives; perhaps never to share an intimate moment, or even a passing moment, again. As I made to push myself up from my seated stupor Babu made eye contact with me and signalled for me to remain seated. Uncertain as to his actions, I remained in my seat until the room was clear of others. Again, our eyes met, and for the first time I realised how piercing was his gaze. And yet, despite his darkened appearance, his eyes were the colour of cobalt. He motioned me forward; I approached and leaned on my haunches.

'You don't belong here,' he said in a rhythmic voice. 'This place is not for you. In here you wander around aimlessly lost in other peoples' dreams. We come to help those who can still be helped. You must leave now before you lose the return path. You must return whilst you still have the memory to return. Go now, and remain true to your longing.'

As soon as Babu had said this, I remembered that for so many days I had forgotten to think about my daughter back at the cottage - how could I have forgotten?! What had impelled me to lose sight of such treasure? It was like leaving behind a pearl of great price when setting out upon a journey. I bowed to Babu and thanked him deeply for his help. Then I hurriedly left the caravanserai and made my way back through the marketplace. In my hurry I had even forgotten to bring with me my bundles of wood. Yet as soon as I had this thought, a new idea entered my mind: had I ever really been a woodcutter?

The throng of market dwellers passed me by. Their animated gestures seemed alien to me now like a carnival of crooked caricatures. Shouts and traders' calls filled the air and mixed with poultry clucks and rank scents. A smorgasbord of smells attacked my senses as I dashed, half-dazed, through the clamouring streets to find the way back to my cottage in the woods.

At each step I took I sensed the cushion of time press against my stomach like a corset closing in. My mind, filtered through this world, existed in a shared collusion. Now, given a poke from an intervening realm, it had begun to relieve the yoke of its consensus reverie. And it was in this state of myriad rapid-firing thoughts that I arrived at my cottage door. Finding it unlocked, I entered.

The same basic cottage as I had remembered it from before. Yet now the place felt empty and cold: no wood-stove burning; no coffee brewing; and no-one else in the cottage. Looking around, I saw no remnants of a life; no clues as to a lived presence. The cottage stood as if a show-house in some open-air museum. A relic of a bygone age, populated by wax figures bent in eternal pose, oblivious to the visitors' gaze. An air of unreality stifled the atmosphere. I could have been standing within a part of a hologram. Each part of us existing as a fragmented section of the overall artificial reality: each cell within me, each splinter of wood, each blade of grass, each bird's plume, a fractal design within some great design. If I had returned to the place where the journey had begun, why was there no resolution? Why was everything so seemingly incomplete?

My memory flickered into filaments of recollection. I had entered the cottage from another place…the room, the old man…and something before…yes, the fountain…

I stepped slowly over to the door of my bedroom and half-pushed it open. I could see nothing through the gap but darkness. I pushed the door open more fully, yet still I could not see clearly into the room. I entered, hesitantly, and stood in gloom until my eyes adjusted to the dark.

The old man looked up from his desk briefly and shuffled his papers. 'You came back,' he said, nonchalantly, as if it was of no concern to him. 'Yet you were lucky. I told you before you left that the laws operate differently out there. I warned you not to forget that what keeps you here will not keep you there. But no matter; you made it back.'

'Yes, I am here now,' I said. I looked around the small office and a fragrance of remembrance seeped into me. The warmth of familiarity was calming. I sensed I was close now to being home.

'Try to remember what you have learnt. It will be difficult at first, yet it will become easier with each attempt,' said the old man, now looking at me with intent. 'We need to make bridges; to re-unite those parts of us which have become lost. We need to be of one realm again. Then we can all go ahead together.'

I nodded my head, trying to focus upon each word and to lock it within me. I knew that I would soon be leaving this place and that I might not remember fully this experience. It was important I retain something. I strained hard to fix each word within me like an anchor.

'Now,' said the old man, pointing towards a door at the other side of the office, 'you may leave. Your presence has been noted should you ever return to this threshold - the dweller will be waiting to guide you once again. That is, if you remember how to return. Please, step out and continue along the garden path.'

The old man looked down into his papers and continued to write, like a doctor who has just dismissed his patient. I walked towards the far door and opened it. Without looking back, I stepped out…

26

It was a new sensation for me; the feeling of diminishing time. Of time slipping through the thinned funnel of a glass timer…of an emerging sense of urgency within a realm where time seemingly did not dwell. Perhaps the urgency was only inside of me; my own timer ticking down to the final minutes. I hurried along the streets with my ragged band of lost incarnates huddled close behind me. The recollection of my longing, of my love for the waitress that once burned in me like a branding iron, was now diminishing. My remembrance was now more of my desire than of the desired object herself…as if I had slipped from a primary yearning into a secondary recollection. And now this too was draining away… seeping out of me no matter how hard I strained to keep it in. And so I walked…with determination, putting each foot in front of the other, in fear that I would suddenly forget all and be stranded in an abyss of amnesia.

Within this city stood the edifice of the diner…a stone monument erected to be my memory-pillar. It awaited me – this I knew. I also sensed that my time to find it was dwindling, and each step counting down to some terrible conclusion.

Yet each block stood tall and unknown to me; each edifice unfamiliar and vacant. I passed by dribs and drabs of blank-eyed people shuffling along in obscurity. A fear arose in me; it was a fear of total anonymity…of being lost even to myself…of ending up a lifeless shell…a hollow whole covered shabbily in flesh.

I kept turning to see if the group of nine were still with me. They were managing to keep a little distance away yet always within a few yards of reach. Perhaps they too had sensed a fear…or a fear in me…I do not know nor care to know. I laboured on like a trench-soldier hunched below the battle lines…

I followed a sense of automatic direction. I felt hunted, as if some unknown force had become wise to my presence…a force that regarded me as an invader…a spy…an infiltrator. And now I was on the run, trying to escape from the very non-air that surrounded us. Everything was alien to me now. A realm constructed from foreign particles…I gulped…the air felt liquid as it slipped down my throat. I choked automatically as if fearing a future moment of suffocation… perhaps the program had discovered me…was now re-writing the very atmosphere to weed me out?

Then I saw her standing on the corner. The grieving lady from the church. She is wearing the same black shawl, her hair in a bun, and she is beckoning for me. Quickly, quickly, I can hear the silent syllables from her eyes. I turn behind and beckon my group on…we have to move now… I walk with greater determination towards the old lady…

When I reach the corner, she is no longer there. Again, I see her standing at the bottom of the street, both hands beckoning now as if urging on a listless child. Through unseen mud I march towards her, feeling a weight of gradual heaviness spread throughout my limbs…pulling me down closer to the ground as if some mysterious gravity had been switched on. When I reach the bottom of the street she is still there. I follow her pointing finger as it reaches out to some exterior destination. I see the sign hanging corrupt and tarnished… the diner stands on the far corner like a flagship.

My group come shuffling up to me. I see them cornered, their eyes weak and fearful, yet still alive with some shimmer of expectancy. The old lady is gone. Together we march towards the diner. It is as if we all collectively sense our destination…some location implanted in us and dimly activated…

In weary minutes, stretched as a long-count, we reach the corner. There is almost no light inside…I push open the door…it needs more force than normal…

27

I make my way down a path towards a central clearing where a stone fountain gushes water. The fountain glistens before me, its spray of wet falling onto the low circular wall.

I walk around the perimeter of the clearing and instinctively choose the path on the far side leading away. I follow the garden path and arrive at a wooden door nestled within a vine-covered stone wall. I reach for the handle…

As I pull the door open I feel a sense of being watched…I turn around and…

…I see a shadowy form standing at the fountain…a sense of familiarity and warmth pervades my body. I smile and beckon the figure towards me…the male form waves back to me and begins to walk in my direction…I feel a sense of relief…and enter through the garden door…

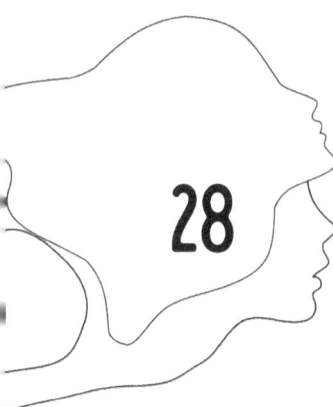

28

The dimness of the diner is fed by two candles burning down to last wax upon the counter. As we enter, a large shadow emerges from the back.

'What yer doing here?!' hollows a bass voice.

'It's me…' I stutter, unable to think of anything else to say. The large shadow of a man steps forward into the penumbra of candlelight and peers at me. Slowly, a grin appears on his face.

'I thought you would never be coming back. Did you find her?'

'Who?' I ask, benumbed.

'The waitress you were looking for. Forgotten already?!' The man bellowed when he spoke.

'No,' I reply meekly. 'I'm here now. Where is the Way?'

'The Way?' The man feigns a look of surprise.

'I know it's through there. I'm going now, and my friends are coming with me,' I say, feeling a new confidence begin to rise in me. The man nods his head.

'Yes,' he replies, 'time remains.' He points to a door behind the bar. 'Through the door into the kitchen and then out through the other door. But you'll be back. I know you will.' The man then smiles in a way which I cannot define, its ambiguity swings between friendliness and the surety of a hunter. I move past the bar and into the kitchen;

the group of nine follow behind.

As soon as we are in the kitchen we walk towards a door at the back. On it is printed, in large bold letters, EMERGENCY EXIT ONLY. I pull down the bar hard and push open…

…blazing light hits my eyes and momentarily stings my retina, blinding my vision…

…I beckon behind me for all to follow…and step through…

… I see a garden path that opens ahead onto a central clearing where a stone fountain gushes water. I make my way down the path towards the low circular wall that surrounds the fountain. Everything here is remarkably clear…vibrant and dancing with colour…in fact, it is too bright for me… I feel dazed in such a place…

…ahead of me, at the end of a path, I see a figure of blazing shades and tints…a strong male form…and a sense of familiarity and warmth enters my body. The figure waves to me and beckons me towards him. I see that he opens a door for me. I wave back to the form and begin to walk. As I do, I turn my head to see the group of nine standing and smiling by the fountain. They are splashing themselves with the fountain spray…they are happy as I walk away… and I feel a sense of relief as I move towards the garden door…

29

The bright glare of the kitchen startles me. The marble surfaces reflect an omniscient coldness to my touch. There is the smell of coffee brewing.

Despite the emptiness of the room I feel a strength in me that is both familiar and yet unfamiliar. It feels like a legacy that has been until now untouched. I sense a welcome home, and yet also a feeling that I stand at the beginning...have always stood at the beginning...

...as if we have been standing at the beginning for so long and now is the time to begin the forward momentum. Awaiting us is the onward journey which is indeed our collective inheritance. Sunk, like deep pearls, the remembrance stirs in us and ignites our longing...

I move towards the gossamer sheets and fall into bed...overtaken by a reverie that snatches at my wakefulness...hoping not to forget...

30

As I open my eyes, I see her standing in the doorway, head tilted in wonder and questions. She is truly my passion-flower anomaly.

'How's the writing going?' she asks.
'Fine,' I say. 'Just fine.'
She walks over to my writing desk and picks up the single sheet of paper. In her delinquently dreamy voice she reads my words to me…

'Our only duty is to keep alive those remembrances that have affected us, and to learn how to say thank you and goodbye. To store within our own silence that which we have loved. Each time we can do this is an act of personal enchantment…

…A new dawn is coming. Then our stories will begin anew. From this moment do I rest, for the future will be lighter. And love will know new colours, new fragrances, others' hearts. And the journey will begin its cycle of renewal, and it will be good.'

Beautiful Traitor Books was founded in 2012 as an independent print-on-demand imprint to provide unusual and inspiring books for the discerning reader.

Our books are works that delve into various domains whether it is books for children, science fiction, social affairs, philosophy, theatre plays, or poetry. We have books translated into Spanish, French, Portuguese, Italian, and Hungarian.

All the books we publish seek to explore innovative and creative ideas. Many of them also tell a good story - stories that have different perspectives on life and on the human condition.

Beautiful Traitor Books is not only about offering the reader entertainment. We also seek to offer something that is like a nutrition; something of value that the reader can take away from the book. Good books function on more than one level. Put simply, we thrive on books that have the capacity to *shift* the reader.

Come and join the conversation – find out more at:

www.beautifultraitorbooks.com